**Praise for the writing of Terri Pray**

*Focused On Love* is an absolute page-turner. The poignant heart-tugging characters touch the heart in such a way that it is hard releasing them once the book is finished. Dani and Steven make such a delightful couple and the way they seek to conquer the odds stacked up against them is well-written. Ms. Pray pens a sharp and intense read that keeps the reader mesmerized.
    -- Linda L., *The Romance Studio,* on *Focused On Love*

*Ettore's Women* is a beautifully written and perhaps deliberately fragmented story of women who work in a brothel. Terri Pray's voice fascinates me. I want to read more.
    -- Catherine H., *Novelspot,* on *Ettore's Woman*

The novel flows extremely well. There is never a dull moment and the sex is blistering hot. *Sweet Deceptions* is a great way to spend a lazy afternoon. Full of intrigue it keeps you wondering what is happening and who did it.
    -- Leyna, *Fallen Angel Reviews,* on *Sweet Deceptions*

...[A]n enjoyable fast read with the premise of being able to unleash the magic within yourself, if you have enough faith.
    -- Aggie Tsirikas, *Just Erotic Romance Reviews,* on *Green Dreams* (Mojocastle Press)

# Curvaeous Heart

## Terri Pray

## Warning

**This book contains sexually explicit scenes and adult language and may be considered offensive to some readers.**

This book contains explicit sexual content and graphic language.

*Curvaeous Heart*

*Published by Under the Moon, LLC Pelican Rapids, MN*

This book is a work of fiction. Any resemblance to actual events, locales or persons, living or dead, is completely coincidental.

*Curvaeous Heart*
ISBN: 978-1-938339-33-2
Copyright © 2016 Terri Pray
Cover Art Copyright @ 2016 Sam and Terri Pray
Editor in Chief: Terri Pray
All rights reserved.

## Dedication

*To my Sam, thank you now and always for your help, love and support.*

# *Chapter One*

*A new week means a new diet, doesn't it?*

Sue glared at the calendar in disgust. Which one would she convince herself to try this time around? There had to be some new fad out there to lose the pounds that had followed her around since teenage years. A few weeks of sweating in the gym, cutting out all the good things in life and for what? So she could look the same at the end of that torturous time and still not fit into the latest backless, strapless, barely there fashions.

It would be another waste of time and money. And she'd still be left dealing with men like Bill at work. So why put herself through all of that?

Between the date and the dream, she'd woken up in a foul mood and the magazines that had been scattered over the table hadn't helped. Skinny models, with barely wafer thin bodies and wearing little more than a few scraps of cloth in the name of fashion certainly hadn't improved her mood.

"Is there something the matter?" Barb patted Sue on the shoulder, her fingers giving a brief reassuring squeeze. "You've been glaring at that calendar for the past ten minutes now. I know you didn't sleep well. I could hear you calling out earlier."

"Nothing much, just... well I've decided to change a few things about myself I just had a bad dream, nasty one. Bill was in it." Sue looked away from the calendar. Whatever happened she wasn't going down that track again. Her body had only just forgiven her for the last series of sessions in the gym. What had she been thinking of? Fast music, toned bodies and with no one willing to walk her through the basics slowly first; her body had screamed murder for nearly ten days after the first class.

"That's just wrong on a dozen different levels. You're really not having a good day of it. Maybe we should have a girl's night out tonight, get your mind off that creep."

"No, I'm not having a good day of it but that's going to change. I can't let things continue like this." A night out on the town? Looking at all the slim things walk off with the only decent men in the place. Just what her ego needed right now.

Not.

"So, what have you got in mind?" Barb moved back through the kitchen, the clink of cups being set down on the counter soon followed by the rich smell of coffee.

"Nothing much. Not as though I've got a boyfriend to plan on celebrating my birthday with, is it?" Another year older, just what she needed.

"Now Sue, don't start knocking yourself again. That's exactly what Bill and men like him want. You're better than that. You always have been."

"Just wish I felt that way sometimes."

"Sue. All right, let's try a different tact then. Are you planning on letting him ruin your birthday?"

"No, of course not. I'll figure something out. I'm just not sure what right now."

Sue frowned as she glanced towards the pot; the smell was tempting at the best of times. Coffee wasn't the best thing she could start the morning off with but if she had one without cream then she would not feel quite so guilt about it.

Damnit. She was doing it again. She had to break that habit if she wanted to stand a chance to change the way she viewed herself. No one else was going to do this for her. God knows she'd been told that often enough.

"Don't tell me, you're going to tip a gallon of milk over Bill the next time he tries one of his fat jokes?" Barb chuckled.

Bill. Now there was a man she could happily kill. "That would depend on if the milk had turned sour yet or not. I wouldn't want to waste good milk. Not when there are so many other uses for it."

"Good point. I'd go for three-month-old eggs personally. Right in the face. Or in a bucket over his head, tipped at the last possible moment just when he realizes what you have in store for him."

The image of rotten eggs sliding down over his annoying face, messing up his carefully dyed hair and that tan he worked on every weekend he had the chance, almost reduced her to a hysterical pile of sobbing woman in the middle of the floor. "I could sell tickets to that little scene. I think half the office would turn out to watch that."

"We'd make a fortune. I think you and I are about the only women he has not tried something on in the office. I swear that bastard knows everything that goes on in the office. Joan caught him rummaging around the boss's office the other day. He claimed that he was in there fixing the computer. Not something I'd believe. That man would not lift a finger to help unless there was something in it for him. Bah, I'm not going to waste the only quiet moments we're going to get until dinner time on that asshole." Barb pushed one of the cups across the table towards Sue. "Come on, sit down, drink up and tell me just what's going on in that head of yours. Because whatever it is it must be important to you as you're frowning."

With the robe wrapped tight about her body, Sue settled down at the table and that same frown still creased her brow. She knew that without even looking in a mirror. Just what had affected her so badly? Bill, the day, the number the scales had revealed before she had stepped out into the kitchen or all the expectations that had been shown by those damn magazines?

She should have known better than to pick them up in the first place. Half the women in the pictures had been airbrushed; the rest, well, they had to starve themselves in order to look like that, nothing else made sense.

"I'm not sure where to begin."

"Well, let's see if I can work this out. It's Monday, start of the month and I know fully well that you spent the weekend muttering every time you flicked through one of those wretched magazines. So I'm betting you were planning on starting a new diet but something has changed your mind." Barb spoke over the rim of the coffee, her long blonde hair caught in a loose pony tail at the nap of her neck, soft blue eyes fixed on her friend's face.

To say Barb was pretty would have been an understatement. And unlike most women Barb did not need to work out, or watch the carbs, calories, or anything else in order to keep herself looking well. It came as naturally to her as breathing did. Right down to instinctively knowing which fashions would look good on her and which were a waste of time.

Just what a woman like Barb was doing sharing an apartment with a woman like Sue had been the talk of the office for the first two years and more. And like all other forms of gossip, the topic occasionally drifted back into favor before being laid to rest again for a few more months when a more interesting subject stumbled into the hapless grasp of the office bobble heads.

"Well, how close am I?"

"Spot on," Sue admitted, curling her fingers about the steaming cup. "I started thinking about all the money I've wasted over the years on those damn diets and gym memberships."

"Well, the gym side of things isn't such a bad idea, but you could take a better attitude towards it, find a class you like instead of living in the gym for six straight weeks. Or jumping up to the top level. Even if you just did one class a week until you got the hang of things it would work. But keep to the low impact stuff."

"Thanks, I thought you'd be happy about my decision." Typical, the one person she had come to rely upon for support and...

"I am, if you gave me the chance to finish what I was trying to tell you then you'd be aware of that." The warm look in Barb's gaze took the sting from her words. "You know I wouldn't do anything to hurt you."

"Oh, I just... never mind, go on with what you were saying then." Heat flushed across her cheeks as Sue fought against the instinct to take an extreme interest in the table top instead of looking at her best friend.

### *Curvaeous Heart*

"I'm trying to tell you that you're fine just the way you are. Sure you're a little heavier than the fashion models but let's be honest here, a stick insect weighs more than those women. I'd be seen as heavy next to them. Needing to firm up, and get into some good habits with exercise is not the same as saying you're ugly, Sue. Just remember that sometime." Barb smiled, nodding towards the coffee cup.

"It's easier to think the worst, even with friends sometimes." Sue admitted, unable to meet her friend's gaze. Ugly was an easy label to deal with -- fat, slob, unattractive -- yes, they all came too easily to mind when she looked in the mirror. Bill would like that, he'd get a kick out of knowing his words hurt, those nasty, snide little comments that wormed their way under her skin. Fuck him. She didn't have to take that. Not anymore. "Sorry, I should have let you finish before jumping like that."

"It's understandable. I know you've been edgy ever since having to deal with Bill. But you'd be better off remembering that not every man, or woman out there, fell from the same branch as that prick."

"I'll try." More than try, or else Bill would not just win in the short term, but for the rest of her life. Not just him, but every man and woman like him. There were enough of them. It wasn't just the ones that tossed comments her way, but the ones that shot those disgusted, or worse, pitying looks when she went shopping, or stopped in a café for a bite to eat.

She knew what they were thinking. That a woman of her size didn't need to have that piece of pie, or a sandwich, that maybe she'd be better off trying to starve herself and eat nothing but grapefruit or whatever the latest fad diet was these days.

What did they know?

Did they really think that if she kept cutting down her food, and cutting it down further, that she'd be able to lose weight? It didn't work that way. The more you cut out, the slower the body worked and the more weight it horded. That was the first mistake she'd ever made as far as trying to conform to fashion had been con-cerned. Fifteen hundred calories had been cut down to a thousand, then eight hundred. By the time Barb had slapped some sense into her she'd gone down to around five hundred a day and had almost keeled over at work.

Not something she'd do again.

"Drink up, you need it, we've got a pretty long day ahead of us today." Barb nodded towards the cup of coffee.

"Don't we always on a Monday?"

# *Chapter Two*

"So, where do we stand?" His father's gaze narrowed on the files scattered across the desk.

Business. Right now, Alan wanted to just shut the files and walk away. "It doesn't make sense except in one way. We have a mole. Just -- well the information that's leaking out doesn't fit with the standard plant situation we've dealt with before."

"In what way?"

"The information that's being leaked is almost random. It's been ranging from bland coffee meetings, to full-fledged deals. Shit, when I have someone asking me what type of paper we've decided to use for the official letters now, or someone asking me if I've hit on the new girl in the office yet because they hear she's a good lay, then I wonder if it's coming from someone on the pay of one of our rivals."

"Great, just what we need right now."

"I'll get to the bottom of it sooner or later. I just don't know where to start. If the leaks made sense, then it would be easier." Who wanted to know what weight paper they used? Or what flavor coffee he preferred to drink? It just didn't make sense, yet some of the information that had filtered back to him appeared to cover trivial matters that no professional office mole would have bothered with.

"So maybe it's nothing more than someone just trying to start trouble for kicks instead of an actual problem."

"It went beyond that the minute they soured the Harper deal for us." Fifty thousand pounds down the drain. Wonderful. Not something he wanted to have to deal with every day. Sure it wasn't huge compared to some projects but it was still enough that he winced every time he thought about it.

"We earned that back within a week."

"That's not the point, Dad! We can't keep brushing off losses like that. How long will it be before this leak blows everything for us?" Alan grabbed one of the papers from his desk. "Look at this! We have three complaints from women who used to work for us about someone stalking them, harassing them via anonymous emails. They claimed it had to tie in with us. I've not been able to find a damn thing that traces back to us."

Neil rubbed his thumb along the edge of his jaw. "And there's nothing conclusive?"

"Just hints, rumors that it could be one of a dozen people currently working for us. I've implemented a new policy though, to be on the safe side. Any visitors are to be escorted in and out of the building from now on. They can sit in the lounge, that's not a problem, but walking through the building will be done with an escort or not at all. It won't stop what's going on, but might help us rule out any outside elements, such as people going into the file rooms, or hanging out in the break room when they have no right to be there."

"It's a start but I don't think you're on the right track, it can't be an outsider."

"I never said it was, Dad. This is just a way of making sure that whoever is behind this is working for us. The first thing any solicitor is going to say is that we didn't check all the options before firing the jerk. So I don't want to end up facing those types of allegations just because we were trying to protect the company."

"Oh, I see." Neil leaned back in the chair and nodded. "Makes sense now you've explained it fully. So what are you doing to stop the rumors flying?"

"I'm keeping information to those who need to know and no one else, as much as possible that is; the problem is that every time I write a memo it passes through a dozen hands. Then it ends up in the file room. Even via email there's no way of knowing for certain just who else sees it. We installed the keystroke program, but that doesn't stop someone calling a friend over to read it on their screen."

"Keystroke?"

"Dad, when are you going to join the digital age? Keystroke records every stroke of a key, or command on a computer and keeps a track of it for us, so we know whose using our time, connection and computer system to goof off."

"Damn, I remember the days when we had to track who was using the phone system to make overseas and long distance calls; that was hard enough to deal with until that new exchange system came in. System X I think they called it. Something BT brought in a good few years ago now."

A slight smile tugged at the corners of Alan's lips. "Keystroke is something like that but for a computer." All right, it wasn't quite the same thing, but his father's knowledge of computers, servers and programs could have been written on the back of a postage stamp. Not that he was unintelligent but for the most part computers didn't interest him, beyond the capability of using them for email and the occasional web search.

"Good, but everyone knows about this program?"

"Yes, Dad. First time we caught someone out with it the word got around. Still, its cut down the wasted online time and productivity has increased." And now this problem had appeared, less than a year after Keystroke had been installed, he couldn't help but wonder what would have happened if he had held off on using it. Would it have caught the person behind their current troubles?

No, he couldn't think like that. It wouldn't help him sort things out now.

"All right, then I'd best get myself back home." Neil Martin pushed to his feet and straightened his jacket.

"Sure, Dad. I'll take care of things here." Or he'd at least make a damn good attempt to. If he ever got his hands on the person behind their latest round of troubles he'd squeeze the life from their scrawny necks.

"And I'll see you on Friday night?"

"The cocktail party, sure."

"With Victoria?"

"Dad ..."

"You can't blame an old man for trying." A wicked grin flashed across his father's face. "Besides, she'd liven the place up a little."

"Dad, for the last time. Stop trying to fix me up. I'm fine. If I want to date someone I'll choose them, is that clear?"

"Sure, son. For now at least. I'll find a way to see you married to a good woman sooner or later. You know I will." Neil smiled and straightened the tie he wore.

"No, I don't. I won't date someone just because you want me to. And the sooner you learn that the easier things will be between us."

"Now, Alan. There's no need to ..."

"Yes, there is." Alan rose slowly and walked around from behind his desk. When was his father going to learn? Trying to coerce him into a date wasn't the sort of thing he tolerated.

"Now, Alan. Listen to me for a minute. I'm not going to put up with this from you."

"Dad, this isn't going to work." Alan frowned and watched his father pace across the office. "I don't care how many wealthy women you try to pair me up with I'm not going to go out with someone based on your thinking that  --  shit, I don't know what you were thinking. Vicky just isn't my style."

"Victoria Shelby comes from a good family and has more than enough money behind her that she wouldn't be looking to leach from the company." Neil Martin scowled and sat down. "I don't know what's wrong with you, Alan. Most men would give their right arm to be seen with Victoria. She and your mother even belong to the same club."

Alan tried not to laugh. His father's temper was showing through his otherwise cultured veneer. Though his father would have denied it, the signs were all too clear to Alan. The carefully practiced B.B.C.  English had slipped in places, granting life to a hint of the

## *Curvaeous Heart*

Scouse accent his father had grown up with. The older man put his feet up on the table and crossed his ankles.

He'd come a long way from the narrow houses of Bootle with their cobbled back alley ways. Strange, it was the twenty-first century and those little places still existed. Had they changed much since his dad was a young man? Or had the basics remained the same? It wasn't the type of place Alan had any desire to go and explore for himself, but at times like this he had to wonder just what it had been like to grow up in such a place.

"I'm not most men, Dad. Never have been, never will be." Alan looked down at the waiting files on his desk. "Oddly enough the work here, getting things back on track, is more important to me than finding some attractive and empty headed bimbo to have on my arm for the right functions."

"Alan!"

* * * * * *

"Well, if she's anything like the last three women you've tried to pair me up with then she doesn't have an original thought in her head. First there was Caroline, who had a hard time deciding what color shoes to wear with her latest outfits. Then Naomi, who had the meanest temper I've ever seen. And let's not forget Ginny who thought the world revolved around her spa appointments."

"So I want to see my son settled down and married to a woman of good breeding. Isn't it about time you did something about giving us grandchildren?"

"Shit, Dad. This isn't the nineteenth century any more. It's the twenty-first. You can't go around trying to match me up with every woman you stumble across. I'm twenty-five for pity's sake. I've got my whole life ahead of me. Why would I want to go looking for a wife right now? I can't even imagine myself as a father."

"Because you need to settle down. Besides, don't you want to still be young enough to raise your children?" Neil brushed a nonexistent piece of fluff off his trouser leg.

"I'm not even sure I want kids." There it was, out there, open on the table. It wasn't exactly the way he'd wanted to tell the old man, but once said it couldn't be taken back. Maybe when the time was right, when he was settled and finally found someone who -- who understood him. Who wanted to explore the type of relationship Alan already knew he needed, then it would be a different matter entirely.

"What!" Neil sat bolt upright, the color draining from his face. "You can't be serious about that. How could you think of not wanting kids? It's a natural part of life, men want heirs."

"I didn't say that, I said I wasn't sure I wanted them. There's a difference. Dad. I'm too young to be worrying about all that."

"You've no idea just how fast life can catch up with you. And when it finally hits you, then you'll regret not finding a wife earlier."

* * * * * *

Well he hadn't wanted it to go this far but there was one threat the old man would have to listen to. "Dad. I am not going to be pushed into a date and the next time you try to fix me up with someone I'll quit the company. Is that clear?"

"Now Alan, there's no need to make irrational threats like that. We both know you wouldn't walk out on the company." His father cracked a half smile.

"That's where you're very much mistaken. I can and I will. If walking out on you, this place and the company as a whole is the only way to get you to see sense and quit your matchmaking schemes then you bet I'll leave the lot behind."

The color drained from his father's face as the senior Martin turned and half paced the room, muttering beneath his breath. Alan tried not to smile, but kept his face, with effort, under control. Walking away from the company, or his father, wouldn't be that easy, but he'd follow through with his threat if that's what it took. If nothing else he'd learned one thing all too well. Never use a threat unless you were willing to see it through to the bitter end.

"Fine. I'll stop asking you to bring a date. But I can't be held responsible for any women approaching you at events. You're a wealthy young man, Alan. That does draw interest."

"And no handing my number on to them either."

"I never did -- all right I did it once but only once. It won't happen again." Neil offered a sheepish smile. "Besides I thought you two would make a cute...."

"Dad!"

"Yes, you're right. Bad idea." Neil glanced up at the clock on the wall. "Shit, I'm going to be late and your Mum will never forgive me."

"Understandable. Give my love to her will you."

"Of course, she'll be expecting you there on Friday night, so don't forget."

"I won't."

How could he. Half the local businesses were going to be there, and if all went well with the meeting earlier that day then there would be some good news to announce. Just as long as the idiot behind the information leaks was caught before then.

* * * * * *

"Mr. Martin?" A slightly balding man peeked his head around the corner of the door. "Steph said you wanted to see me?"

Alan frowned, his gaze narrowing on the doorway. Had he told his secretary to let anyone in? The meeting with his father had left him unsettled and it took him a moment to put his thoughts in order. "Charlie? Ah, yes. Sorry I'd forgotten you were -- never mind, come in."

The middle aged man slipped into the room, closing the door behind him. With an overly confident stride Charlie straightened his hair, hiding the bald spot before speaking. "If it's about the sales reports I know I'm running a day or so late, but I'll have them ready for Friday."

"That won't be good enough. I'll need them no later than Wednesday night and you should have had them on my desk last week, at the very latest. I don't like the way you've been getting sloppy about these things." Charlie Welch, the man had become a thorn in his side of late, but in nothing that he could actually fire the idiot for. When pushed he did do the work, but it was seldom on time.

Of course there were always excuses.

His computer at home crashed, which was where he was doing the extra work, without billing the company for it of course. Or the email didn't go through. He'd thought he'd already sent it, or it was the copier machines fault for playing up at the wrong moment. He'd used every excuse short of the dog eating his homework, and still expected people to believe him.

"I'm not sure that will be possible without putting in some extra hours, Mr. Martin." Charlie smiled and slipped his hands into his pockets. "I've been running into a few problems with the accounting software and ..."

"You've had more than enough time, and we both know it."

"Now, Mr. Martin, you know I'll be able to do the work if I can just focus on that instead of a dozen other matters at the same time." He gave a half shrug.

"Maybe if you did your work instead of doing three other things, and not chasing half the women in the office then you'd be on time."

"Can I help it if they find me attractive, sir?"

"Cut the crap, Charlie. I'm not in the mood for games. If you don't have that report to me by Wednesday, then I'll fire you. It's as simple as that. I'm done with your late reports, your lame answers and your wasting company time by chasing every new woman who starts work here. Don't think I haven't noticed. I deal with the complaints."

### *Curvaeous Heart*

Charlie scowled and took a step back, a slight tremble running through his shoulders. "Who are you going to believe, Alan? Some kid that just started working here, or a man who's put the best part of ten years into this place? I was here when you were still in college! Your father knows the level of work I do, what I'm capable of and ..."

"And that's the only reason you haven't been fired already. If I even catch a hint of any more nonsense from you I'll have you moved to our secondary location." No one wanted to move out of the new building into the older and smaller unit that they still used for one or two of the smaller operations.

"You can't pull this shit on me, Alan. You don't have the right."

A cold hand clutched about Alan's heart as he stood up, pushing back from behind the desk. "Are you trying to tell me what I can and cannot do within my own company?"

Charlie took three quick steps backwards and blanched. "No, I'm sorry. I don't mean it that way. I wasn't thinking clearly. I'm sorry sir, I've been under a lot of stress lately. I spoke without thinking."

Alan glanced at the computer screen, the papers across his desk, the work that he knew had to be done before Friday. Would firing him now do any real good? He'd only have to pass the work onto someone else and they'd have to begin it from scratch. Not a good situation, not with the limited time he had to work with.

But it would have felt so damn good to be rid of the man.

"I'll have the report to you on time, Alan. You have to give me the chance to prove that to you."

Funny how he went from *Mr. Martin* to Alan in the span of a couple of minutes. As if he had the right to -- no it wasn't worth the argument. Not when there were other, more important things to attend to.

"This is your last chance, Charlie. I won't tolerate any further fuck-ups from you. I don't care how long you've been working for the company if you can't do the job, on time, then I won't have you working here."

For a moment, less than a heartbeat, something flickered across Charlie's face. A flash so brief that Alan almost missed it as the other man's eyes narrowed, darkened and his jaw clenched, only to fade just as quickly into a mask of meek acceptance.

"Understandable, anything you say. The report will be with you on time, on Wednesday, no later than that. You have my word on it."

# *Chapter Three*

"Sue, get your fat ass out of the way, I'm trying to get past here." Bill smirked, his hands filled with an armload of packages. "I can't do my job if you're just going to stand there in the way blocking the corridor."

Flame danced across her cheeks, her hands clenching into tight fists as a dozen retorts tried to bubble into life. She had taken just about all she was prepared to from him today, or any other day for that matter, but it didn't mean she needed to sink to his level. "There's plenty of room, I don't see why you're making such a fuss."

"Sure there would be, if you weren't taking up the space. Now get out of the damn way, fatty. I've got too much to do today and it's bad enough that I have to deal with you at the pub. I'm surprised you haven't been banned by now. A bitch like you is going to break the bar stools before much longer."

Her hands clenched quickly. Images of smashing her fist into his face, seeing the blood splatter across the walls quickly died as common sense took control.

How much trouble would she get in if she hit him? Fired, that was certain, maybe some time in jail for assault. No, the bastard wasn't worth it. Normally she would have let him get away with it, crammed her body against the wall and then ignored the elbow in her breasts or the phantom grab of flesh when he deliberately pressed against her on the way past.

Not this time. Not with the memory of her conversation with Barb still fresh in her mind.

"What's up, Bill? Haven't you been laid in a while?"

The color drained from his face, lips moving silently. In a heartbeat he had turned from the office stud into a fish out of water.

"Ah, I hit the mark there didn't I?" She pressed, unwilling to give up the advantage she had stumbled into. Had no one tried this tactic with him before? From the look on his face it certainly appeared that way. "You've been so busy moving from one woman to the next in the office that you've now gone through every available option. That leaves Barb and me, neither of whom would have you if you were the last man on the planet. So you're desperate now and trying to scrape the bottom of the barrel? Don't tell me you think it turns me on to be insulted by someone like you on a daily basis? I'm a large woman, in all ways, and that includes my level of intelligence."

A low giggle drifted into the corridor from a nearby office door. No calls for help, or for her to stop, no mocking little looks her way. Whoever it was had giggled approved of the little scene as it played out in the brightly lit hallway.

Good.

"You're only saying that because I've never asked you out." He finally stuttered.

"No, you just cop a feel every chance you get. I guess I'm not that unattractive to you, except you've backed yourself into a corner with me, haven't you? All those snide remarks, the jabs, elbows in the stomach. So you're now trying to figure out what to do, aren't you?"

"A woman like you should be grateful that I'd give you a second look." He snarled, fingers tightening on the boxes he held. "You should be thanking me for the attention. Not like you get it from anywhere else. I bet you've not had a man between your thighs in years. You should hear what my mates and I think about your sex life, when you do get it. What happens? The man vanishes into that cavern of yours never to be seen again?"

"No woman wants the type of attention you enjoy giving them. You're no better than the common lounge lizard, but I doubt you have the courage to go and try and meet women outside of work. Oh you're pretty enough, in that cover boy type of way, but you're about as shallow as a baby paddling pool. Three minutes with you outside of work and a woman would quickly find out just what type of would be man you really are. And that's what's now happened. You've run out of options so it's back to buying cheap porno until the next new arrival in the office. Unless of course one of your previous conquests warns her before you manage to get your hooks into her."

"Bitch."

Powerful. His wide-eyed look, the way his lips flapped for a moment before he tried to speak and his constant change of color across his face from washed out to bright red brought with it a feeling of power she had never experienced before

"If being a bitch means I don't stand meekly by while you throw insults my way just because you wouldn't know what to do with a woman in a real situation then by all means I'll gladly take that title and wear it proudly." God, why hadn't she tried this before? The way he half cringed back with each new word that spilled from her lips, the horror flickering across his gaze both added to the new swell of confidence that bubbled through her being.

"You can't talk to me like this, it's... it's harassment. Sexual harassment!" He stammered, looking around the corridor for signs of someone that would be willing to help. "I could have you fired for that. So you better fucking watch your mouth, slut. I'll drag you through a hearing the first chance I get. Just you wait. They'll fire your ass and I'll drink to you being sacked, knowing you can't even afford a shandy."

"And how many women in the office would come forward with stories of what you've pulled on them, not to mention the witnesses who've seen and heard some of the things you've done to me. Who do you think is going to get into more trouble?" If she did not back down, if she kept on the offensive then she would be fine. But one sign of weakness and the whole situation would backfire on her.

"No one would believe you."

"So why are you backing away? You know they'll speak up, we've all seen what you can do. Shit, most of the women here have been on the receiving end of your little stunts."

"I..." The color, what little had been left, now faded from his skin.

"Get out of here Bill, before I decide to see just how many of the women here would like to see you hauled up before the boss." She took a step towards him, pressing the point home. "Go, now! Before I lose my temper with you."

Bill fell silent, taking a step away from her before turning and hurrying back down the corridor without another word.

Damn, that had felt good. Had he really always been that spineless? Shit, if she'd known that she'd have taken action against the idiot months ago. Maybe what he really needed was a strong woman to show him the error of his ways?

A sudden image of Bill down on his hands and knees, licking the boots of some black leather dressed dominatrix brought an instant smile to her lips. Now that was something she might well have paid to see.

And she wouldn't have been the only one.

If the thought hadn't truly disgusted her then she'd have imagined Bill on his hands and knees, licking at her boots, begging to be paddled like a naughty slave from one of her erotic novels.

"I've been waiting for someone to take that sleaze down now for the past few months." A pair of wide brown eyes peeked out from behind the door that had been the source of the giggle. "He's been working his way through the women here and I was worried he might try and go for seconds with a few of us."

"Ann isn't it?" Sue moved a little closer and then walked into the small side office when the other woman opened the door up fully.

"Yes, and you're Sue? From accounts?"

Sue nodded, settling down on the edge of the cluttered desk. "You've had a run in with him? Bill, I mean."

"Several." The soft-eyed woman nodded a little. Five-six at most, with pale skin and long brown hair and no older than twenty-eight or -nine, Ann looked more like a demure school teacher than a secretary of a busy firm. Unlike so many of her age group she had chosen high-necked shirts, long skirts and flat shoes. No slave to fashion here, but a sensible woman who knew what worked for her chosen career. "He chased me for three months before I finally agree to go out with him. Always so helpful, until he got what he wanted then I didn't exist. I can't believe I was that stupid, falling for his lines and his games."

Typical of the man, the same story she had heard from a dozen different women in the past few years. "He does that, but normally it doesn't take him so long to get a woman to agree."

"Barb warned me when I first arrived to give him a wide berth."

"Good." Okay, that part made sense, but then had she given in? "What made you change your mind about him? Something must have happened for you to end up going out with Bill."

"He's smart. He played on a few weaknesses of mine. I can't believe that I fell for it, but he did the whole *prince charming* routine. I just thought, well, that maybe he and Barb had gone out and she was doing the ex-girlfriend routine. I loved what you did to him out there, but I'm not sure it was such a good idea. He won't let you get away with it you know."

"Well no one has ever denied that about him, but what difference did it make with you?" Get away with it? She had already managed that part of the plan. Bill had all but run back down the corridor and had shown no signs of coming back at her. Sue watched Ann closely, waiting to learn a little more about the man she had sent fleeing down the hallway, face crimson.

"He was nice around me, didn't set off any alarm bells, helped out a lot. If I needed anything he was right there, getting things fixed for me. I guess I bought into the game." Twin points of heat flared in the young woman's cheeks as she sucked in her bottom lip. A soft quiver rippled through her words, tiny lines tightening around the corners of her eyes and lips. "Foolish I know, I should have listened to my gut and kept away from him. Shit, I really did think Barb was either jealous or there was something else going on. It serves me right for trusting the prick, even for a short while."

"We all make mistakes." Sue tried to reassure her. "You aren't the first to fall for it. Honestly, if he'd been nice to me when I first started working here I might have made the same mistake, so please, don't beat yourself up over him. He's just not worth it."

"Yeah, and mine ended up on the Net. I'm betting that's what will happen with your run in with him, only he'll twist it. He always does." Ann frowned, shaking her head. Her lips pressed into a tight, thin line, jaw set. "That bastard always twists things when he posts them up though."

Her jaw tightened, frown deepening across her brow. "End up on the Net? What do you mean by that?"

"A blog, he has one, spills everything across it. I thought you knew? It's one of those online journal things." Ann explained, glancing towards the door as she did so. "You really didn't know about his blog? He writes in it every day. Some of the things he puts there are sickening."

"No, who else knows about this blog thing of his?" Her heart sank, what had he posted to that thing? Lies, slander, vicious rumors that would only offer further hurt to the women in the office?

"I just assumed everyone did." She shrugged a little, not meeting Sue's gaze. "I stumbled across it when he took me around to his place that night. I think he forgot to turn the computer off and when I nudged the mouse the screen came up. Luckily he didn't notice and I took a note of the address so I could read It when I had the chance. I almost regretted I'd done that the first time I read the blasted thing. He's sick you know, twisted and cold."

Her throat tightened. Had that been part of what Bill had been doing when he had been caught rooting around the office? If he had been posting inside information on what was going on at work he could easily now face legal action from the company.

"How much does he put up there?"

"Everything. The only thing he doesn't do is post his name to it.

## *Curvaeous Heart*

He has it listed up as 'A Real Man'. I couldn't believe he was doing that at first, then I kept going back, looking up what he was posting, the feedback, he's on some sort of network, web ring I think they call them, of other men doing the same thing. Spilling the dirt on the women they work with. Not just that either, but family secrets, work information, it's sick some of the posts you read there." Ann spoke quickly, her face flushed then drained of color once more. "I'm sorry, I really thought everyone already knew about this. God, you should see some of the crap he's come up with over the past couple of months."

"Shit." Sue grasped the edge of the desk. It was just the sort of thing Bill would pull, it matched his ego. Just what lies he had been spreading on the blog she couldn't be sure of but the last thing she was about to do was let the asshole get away with it, not after managing to stand up to him in the corridor.

*Hold on a minute, just what in hell's name do I think I'm doing? I can't take him on like this. It's one thing to give him a little payback here, but what do I know about dealing with blogger postings?*

About the same as she'd known about working a computer when she'd first started work, but she'd learned that pretty quickly. Besides, didn't the police trace problems on the Net all the time?

*Yes and they're the police. They have resources I don't have at all. This isn't some game -- but I can't just sit back and let him get away with this.*

"I need the address. I can't just sit back and let this happen."

## *Chapter Four*

"Alan! Just what's going on around here? That damn secretary insisted that I be escorted up here. I know everyone who works here by now and I've never been made to feel so distrusted in my entire life."

His heart dropped as the woman's voice shattered the peace and quiet of his office. Hadn't he made it clear to his father that he didn't want to date the blasted woman? "Victoria, what are you doing here?"

"Well is that all the hello I'm going to get? Aren't you even going to look at me?" The little girl pout voice she did so well dripped into every word. "I came all this way to see you, the least you can do is spend a little time with me."

"I'm a little busy right now, so what is it you..." He turned, his breath catching in the back of his throat as his gaze fixed on her.

At five foot eleven Victoria was one of the few women who could, with the aid of heels, look him directly in the eyes. But that wasn't what stopped him in his tracks now.

Her deep green eyes sparkled, a mane of blonde hair fell loose over her shoulders and the long fur coat she had worn now pooled about her feet leaving her standing in his office wearing nothing but a black silk teddy, stiletto heels and a pair of black hold-up stockings. Her full breasts pressed against the lace edged silk, and even with the teddy covering them he could easily make out her tight, erect nipples.

"What the fuck." His balls tightened, a rush of blood and heat thickened his cock as he stared at her. God, he didn't need this right now.

*So stop and enjoy the view a while. Come on, a free show walks into your office and you're complaining?*

"That sounds about right to me," she stepped away from the

pile of silken fur on the floor. "In fact a good long fuck is exactly what I had in mind."

"Are you insane? Someone could walk in!" He glanced towards the door. If this got out he'd be dealing with shit for weeks to come. He didn't need the trouble, the rumors and sly smiles, not on top of everything else he was dealing with.

"I wouldn't worry about it. I've locked the door and I let your secretary know that we had some business matters to attend to. And I'm right, aren't I? There are a dozen small details we need to go over before Friday. You are coming to pick me up for the party aren't you?"

"No, and I already told my father to stop trying to push us together. I'm not interested." Well part of him wasn't at least.

"Oh, then why is your cock saying differently?" She reached out, brushing her fingertips along the outline of his stubborn erection.

"Look, there is a half-naked woman standing in the middle of the office; of course I'm going to get a hard on, but I'm not going to let my body dictate my actions." The words sounded good, and for the most part he meant them, but when she closed her fingers around the head of his cock through his pants, reason fled.

Victoria leaned forward, brushing her lips across his. "So are you going to stand there with a hard on, or do something about it?"

He leaned back against the desk, clutching the wood. Shit. He couldn't. This wasn't the sort of thing he should be doing. He'd made it clear that he didn't want anything to do with the woman. But each squeeze of her fingers around his treacherous erection made it harder to pull away from her.

He groaned into her mouth, barely aware of her free hand tugging at the tail of his shirt, pulling it free from his pants. His cock ached in her grip, his balls tight and heavy as he pressed back against the edge of the desk. The small voice of reason that screamed at him to push her away found itself gagged by a louder voice, one that demanded he give into Victoria's touch.

"You've kept me at arms-length for too long, lover. All those little hints you kept ignoring. The cards, the messages, I've never met a man like you before, one so determined not to give in. I can't have that." She nibbled her way down his neck, licking along the line of his collar. Her breasts pressed against his chest, even through the shirt and teddy he could feel her nipples, an erotic trail left by heated, hardened flesh, burned into his skin.

*Can't have a man saying no to her? Is that what this is about? I'm a conquest to her?*

Her free hand traced around the edge of his pants, now that his shirt had been pulled free, and opened his belt, unbuttoning his fly a moment later.

*I don't want this -- shit, who am I kidding. Yes I do.*

She tugged down his zipper, releasing her hold on his cock only long enough to pull down his pants and briefs before she wrapped her hand back around his now naked cock.

"Vicky..." He groaned, formality lost in the haze of pleasure. "Don't."

"Why not?" She whispered, easing down onto her knees until her lips were little more than a breath away from his cock.

"Because I -- God!" He arched up from the edge of the desk as her lips wrapped about the head of his cock. "Shit!"

Her tongue wrapped around his cock, one hand cupped his balls and each new touch of her tongue, or gentle caress around his heavy sac, sent a new wave of pleasure through his body. His thighs tightened; heat, sensual heat suckled on his cock, each new tug pushed him further, higher, further away from the small voice of reason.

One finger pressed fully behind his sac, rubbing that tiny, sensitive hidden spot that sent jolts through his body that he couldn't ignore. Pressure, thick, demanding pressure throbbed in the pit of his stomach and for a moment he thought he'd lose control in her mouth. But without warning she pulled away and rocked back up to her feet.

"You want me." She leaned in, stripping his shirt and tie from his body. "So we're going to do something about it, aren't we? In fact, I'm going to ride you, Alan. You'd like that wouldn't you?"

"No!" the word slipped free. Anger bubbled up from the pit of his stomach, pushing aside the desire that had taken control of him.

Victoria leaned in close, licking softly across his lips. "And just how are you going to stop me? I know what your body wants."

It took every ounce of self-control he had in order not to growl at her. Alan pressed his hands against her shoulder, his knuckles white as he tried not to dig his fingers into her flesh. "I will not be ruled by my body, and if you think you can force me to fuck you, you've got another thing coming."

"You arrogant son of a bitch! You think you can turn me down?"

Standing there, arguing with the woman, with his pants down around his ankles wasn't exactly what he had originally planned for his day. "You walk into my office, half strip off, and start trying to seduce me, then think I'm going to meekly go along with whatever you want? Why? Because I'm some testosterone-driven male who doesn't think beyond sticking his cock in the first available hole that comes along?" He reached down long enough to pull his pants back up.

"No man turns me down!" Her voice went up an octave.

"Hm, you know. I'm pretty sure that's what I'm doing." He re-fastened his belt. His balls ached, it didn't matter that his cock had softened the minute he'd realized just how far she was willing to push things. The desire had been real, and his balls now reminded him just how badly he'd wanted to fuck her.

Victoria growled. "Bastard!"

"No, my parents were actually married for a good two years before I came along, so I can honestly say that whilst I may be an asshole, I'm not a bastard. Now get the fuck out of my office before I call security."

Victoria shook her head and turned, walking back to her coat on shaky legs. "You're not normal, or you're gay. That's it. Isn't it? You're gay! Has to be the answer, no way a straight man would turn down a chance at this."

Alan almost laughed, but swallowed the sound just in time.

"Bloody queer. I knew there was something about you the first day we met. I should have stayed clear. Perfect track record until you came into my life."

*Interesting, and here was I thinking she'd walked, no, stormed her way into my life.*

"I suggest you leave, now. In fact, I insist on it." He leaned back over his desk and thumbed the intercom that he knew would be answered by the main reception. "Steph, please come up to my office and escort Victoria out. Also I want it noted by the front desk that she is not welcome here again unless with prior clearance through me."

"Yes, sir. On my way back up." The young woman barely managed to keep the surprise from her voice.

"Now, you have about three minutes to wrap back up before she arrives, and I suggest fixing your makeup. Your lipstick is smeared."

Alan buttoned up his shirt and tucked it back into his pants fully, not even looking up when Victoria left. No, he wasn't gay. He just wanted a woman with -- well -- curves. Real ones, the type he could hold tight and not feel as if they would break in his grasp. A woman who knew how to stand her ground without having to bully a man.

He just hadn't filled her in on the entire truth of the matter.

He liked women with curves, substance to them.

It didn't matter that the rest of the world seemed to think that women like Victoria were the height of beauty, that they should be able to arouse any hot-blooded man within a hundred-meter radius. They just weren't his type and never would be.

# *Chapter Five*

"Are you sure this is a good idea?" Sue murmured as they sat in the large foyer. Her stomach knotted, rolled, then knotted again as she struggled to keep from being sick. "He might think we're nuts, and have us escorted out, or just laugh in our faces. Neither of us need to be out of work right now either."

She could see it now, some high powered executive all dressed up in a flashy suit, staring back at her across a well-polished desk. If they were lucky they'd just be asked to leave and not end up with insults, laughter, or accusations of this being some sort of prank thrown at them.

"Well it was your idea in the first place."

"Barb!"

"I'm only telling the truth. I think it's a good idea, but it was still yours. Now we can follow it through or head for home, either way I'll support you but I won't make the choice for you."

Great, just what she needed.

Sue took a long slow look around the foyer. The chairs weren't bad, better than the scruffy looking things that had been set out in their office, but then again Martin's Enterprises looked as though they were doing well. The front desk hid behind a raised counter, the honey wood polished to the same high sheen that glistened from the floors.

Instead of a drinks dispenser that ate money, a small refreshment area had been set up in the corner, complete with two coffee pots, small pots of half-and-half in the little tubs, and four different types of sweeteners in their colored packets in the little pottery dishes.

A dozen framed photographs decorated the wall, with small plaques under the pictures. Each one was a member of either the Martin family, or their inner circle from what she had been able to make out so far, but one in particular kept drawing her attention.

A man with the name Alan Martin inscribed on the brass plate beneath the frame.

Dark hair, midnight eyes, and a smile that she couldn't quite ignore despite the hint of cockiness that gleamed in his piercing gaze. A man like that probably had every woman in the office panting after him, but that didn't stop her from looking. And perhaps dreaming.

"How much money do you think they spent on this place?" Barb leaned in close and whispered.

"More on the foyer than they did on the entire main office floor of our building." Sue grinned and finally looked away from the picture. All right, so their boss wasn't a bad person, but he did squeeze the pennies tight enough to hear them squeak. "And did you take a good look at the coffee set up?"

"Don't need to, it smells wonderful. Must be one of those nice flavored coffees."

If her stomach hadn't already been involved in a sea battle that left her stomach complaining with every breath, Sue might have risked trying a cup. "How long do you think they'll keep us waiting?"

"Just take a deep breath and focus. We'll get to see him, her, whoever it is they'll let us talk to, and then we can head back for work. Even if they don't take any action at least we can say that we tried."

Would that be enough?

"And if they don't do anything?"

"That's up to them. We can try and do something about Bill, but the others  --  well that's down to our employers. Not us. We can't force people to take action. Maybe Ann's brother will help us, if she calms down enough to tell him. He's bound to have contacts that will be able to track these jerks down. Or we try contacting the women mentioned on the blogs then raise some cash and hire a private detective?" Barb kept her voice low and rested her elbows on her thighs, her chin cupped within her hands.

"Long shot, but it's an option we can look at if we have to." Not the way she wanted to go with it. How many women had been hurt by that ring of hateful men? What did they think they were doing anyway? Just getting some cheap thrills in? Or did they really think they were on top of the game, able to control the world around them by putting those nasty posts up?

Had Bill been the one who had started the whole thing? Or had he just jumped on the bandwagon?

God, sometimes she just wanted to wrap her hands around that bloody man's throat and squeeze until his face turned blue.

"Mr. Martin will see you now." The receptionist slipped out from behind the desk, her low heels barely making a sound on the polished wood floor. "If you'd like to follow me?"

Barb glanced over, the look in her wide eyes giving life to the same question that now rang through Sue's mind. They were being taken to see the owner? Over a rumor? After just walking into the building? All right, either they had lucked out or they were about to be laughed off the face of the planet.

"*The* Mr. Martin?" Sue tried not to stammer as she hurried after the receptionist. The one she'd been ogling on the wall? Or his father? "I wasn't expecting that. I thought we'd just go and talk to someone in..."

"Mr. Martin Junior. Alan Martin." The young woman glanced back over her shoulder then thumbed the button. "I'll walk up with you, it's become policy that all visitors are now escorted through the building."

Why though? Sue nodded and followed the receptionist into the elevator. Had something happened to increase security in the building?

"So where do you two work?" The young woman stepped back from the elevator door. "I'm Stephanie by the way."

"The other building." Barb explained.

"Ah, yes. Small place, nice though, at least from what I've heard." The elevator hummed into life with little more than a soft jerk. "I wasn't aware we had any business matters that needed to be brought over personally, though. Normally we handle anything by phone or computer."

Sue shook her head slightly, catching Barb's attention for a brief moment. The last thing they needed was the story being spread around the office before everything spiraled out of control. God, what were they doing here? It wouldn't take long before they were escorted back out of the building and...

"Well, you know how it can work. It's hard to keep track of who is doing business, or when things are social calls, or just catching up on old times." Barb flashed a confident smile at Stephanie.

"Good point." The elevator stuttered to a halt. "Here we are. I have to escort you right to the door. It's a pain but if I don't I'll end up with a mark on my record. Not something I want."

Odd indeed. Most places just signed people in and out of the building. Sue tried not to frown but could feel the lines furrow across her brow.

"So what's he like?" Barb took the lead through the corridor.

"Alan Martin? Good man, easy to talk to, and gets along with most here. He takes an interest in most things in the company but doesn't lord it over the rest of us. Not the normal sort of son-of-the-boss type." Stephanie smiled, a soft flush of heat shimmering over her cheeks. "Not to mention he's definitely on the cute side of things. You'd expect a man in his position to try and make a pass at the occasional woman here, but no, he keeps his hands to himself."

Great, just what she needed, a handsome son of the boss to deal with. It didn't matter that Stephanie claimed the man played by the rules; men with power grabbed, took advantage, and that was just how life worked. Sue tugged on her blouse, trying to straighten up a little more. At least he would focus most of his attentions on Barb, which might give her the chance to try and put her thoughts in order.

"Well here you go," Stephanie tapped on the door. "Mr. Martin?"

"Come in." The rich, deep voice filtered past the closed door.

## Curvaeous Heart

Stephanie pushed the door open and walked in. "Sue Night and Barbara Haven to see you, Mr. Martin."

"Yes I know, thanks Steph. I'll take it from here." A pair of dark eyes looked up from across the mahogany table. "I'll buzz you when they need an escort out."

Which would be in about five minutes from the way Sue's gut knotted. All right, maybe ten if he was in a good mood; she was a fool for even attempting this.

"Please, sit down." Alan Martin stood up, a warm smile chasing away Sue's doubts for a moment. Now there was a man she could dream about. Tall, easily over six feet, broad shoulders but not enough to fit the rugby player image, and short cut jet black hair. Her gaze played down over his body, to the slight narrowing of his waist. A red, soft cotton shirt clung to his chest and vanished under the black brushed material of his suit pants.

Sue tried not to suck in her bottom lip as she took in every inch of the man they had now been left alone with. He would have looked perfectly at home on the cover of a fashion magazine.

"Thanks." Barb settled into one of the three chairs that had been set in front of the desk.

"The chairs won't bite." He turned the full force of a devastating smile on Sue.

"Er, yes, I know. Sorry." Heat flushed across her cheeks as she sat down.

"Nervous?"

"A little." Sue admitted.

"Sue thinks you'll laugh us out of the office." Barb smiled. "I've tried to tell her that it won't happen, but she's a little nervous."

Sue barely suppressed a groan. Why say that? "It's just a lot to deal with, that's all."

"Well, why don't you tell me what brought you here?" Alan settled on the edge of the desk rather than taking the third chair. "And I don't bite. Well, not often." He flashed another grin, turning his attention fully on Sue. "Unless you ask me really nicely."

Was he flirting with her?

No, of course not. Why would he do that when Barb was in the room? It didn't make any sense. Still, she squirmed on the chair, her thighs pressed tightly together beneath her skirt. Her stomach tightened, a warmth played through her inner walls and for a moment the years stripped away.

No, he was just being polite. That's all it was.

And she was letting her imagination run away with her. That's what she deserved after spending all that time staring at his picture. But at least now she had a voice to go with the image, and together they'd make a delicious package for her next set of dreams.

"There's someone in the company keeping a blog and putting out sensitive material about the company onto the Net." She blurted out the words and tried to break away from his gaze at the same time.

His face instantly hardened. "I see. And just what makes you think it's someone in the company and not a person picking up information on the street?"

There it was, the game face. Tiny lines had narrowed around the corners of his eyes, the muscles across his shoulders tightened.

"Because the information has to come from inside, it's too detailed. The man behind it also lists women in the company he's had sex with, as well as others outside of work, where he scores them or scores their abilities in bed." Sue struggled to keep the stutter from her voice, but the more she spoke the harder it became. "He -- I mean I think he -- well he could damage your company. There was a post -- on the blog -- that spoke of a deal you have in the making with Barnes and Locus. There are a lot of people involved in the ring, all of them put information about the companies they work for but they use codes. Well, initials really. If I hadn't already worked out the code from one person's blog it might have taken me a little longer to work things out."

"That meeting is common knowledge." Alan shrugged though the tension didn't ease from his face. "So I'm not sure what the problem is."

"Is it common knowledge that you will be at the meeting and it's due to take place tomorrow morning at the Royal Hotel? Ten, I think, is the time you're supposed to be there, and it's not a discussion about a possible arrangement, but you're signing the papers." There is was, all the information now laid out on the table for him. What he did next was entirely up to him, but at least they'd taken the time to warn the company.

"Shit!" He slid off the corner of the table. "You're telling me this is all on a blog? Sprawled out across the Net for anyone to see?" His voice went from a calm, conversational tone, to a near yell. "How in hell's name did they get that level of detail? Are you sure it's about this comp -- never mind. Of course you are or you wouldn't be here. All right, fine. I just need a minute to think this through. Bollox. This could blow the entire meeting out of the water."

Sue nodded and tried not to wince. His jaw clenched, full, sensual lips pressed into a tight, thin line. "I'm sorry."

"What for? Unless you're behind the posts." He growled.

"What?" Her hands tightened on the arms of the chair.

"No, that doesn't make sense, you'd not be here if you were involved in this. But I do want to know how you found out about the post, and this ring of bloggers and just what they're up to."

Sue shifted in the chair.

"I'm not sure we can go into all of that right now." Barb began to explain. "There are some hurt feelings involved and a couple of people who I don't feel comfortable..."

"I want the information." He turned to face Barb. "And I don't take well to being told no. So when I tell you to fill me in on the details then that's exactly what you will do."

"I'm sorry but..."

"Barbara, that's your name isn't it? Well, Barbara, I am not asking you, I'm telling you."

"Now hold on one damn minute. You might be the son of the boss here but we don't belong to you. Shit, we didn't have to come to you with this information and you sure as hell don't have any right to treat us like this. So go ahead, fire me. I don't care. I don't want to work for someone who acts like this." Sue gave a sharp wave at Barb before her friend could say anything further.

He blinked and took a step back. "Well if you just gave me the information I need then it would be a different matter."

Sue pushed up from the chair, her hands clenched into tight fists. "I'm sorry we ever came to see you. Barb, I think we should leave. It appears that Mr. Martin needs a lesson in basic manners. Obviously we both have better things to do than pander to his every need."

A smile twitched at the corners of Barbara's lips, and a mischievous light danced within her eyes. "You may well be right. Perhaps we made a mistake in trying to help him."

"Now hold on a damn minute. You can't just leave like that. I need more information." Alan frowned, the growl little more than a memory in his voice.

Sue turned back to look at him. "Then maybe you should remember that shouting, growling, and making demands might be a way to get information from some people, but unlike them I'm not a coward who will back down to an angry child."

Alan blanched.

"So we will see ourselves out, or you can call down for Stephanie to escort us out, either one works for me." Her heart raced beneath her rib cage, her lungs burned, and yet despite the rolling stomach, the quiver in her legs and the way his dark, wonderful eyes, narrowed on her face, she held her ground.

Had anyone ever stood up to him before?

"Did you just call me a child?"

"Damn right I did. You're acting like one. And here I thought you were a businessman who knew how to handle men and women. Instead I find a boy trying to make demands of people who went out of their way to help him." Sue turned and took a step towards the door.

## *Curvaeous Heart*

She made it as far as putting her hand on the doorknob before he spoke again.

"Look, I'm sorry. I just -- can we start again?"

"Are you going to accept that I'm not going to disclose sensitive information without the permission of those involved?"

One strong hand rested lightly on her shoulder. "Yes."

A shiver ran through her body under his touch. God, she didn't need to deal with this right now. Yes he was handsome, and spirited, the way his eyes flashed as he shifted from one emotion to the next was bewitching, but she wasn't here to flirt with the man. Besides, even that hadn't been serious.

"And you promise there will be no more growling, or giving orders?" What would it be like to lean against his hand, and feel his touch fully?

"The giving orders I can promise, the growling -- well all I can do there is try."

Sue took a deep breath and turned to face him. His full sensual lips curved into a smile as he leaned closer. Her skin tingled, nipples crinkling into fine points beneath her blouse. No, she had to keep this under control. Letting him see how she was affected by him would be a mistake.

"Are you saying you have a slight temper issue?"

"Only on matters I feel passionately about." His breath caressed her face. "And I'm afraid when it comes to matters of business, I'm very passionate indeed."

*Oh, I bet you are.*

"Fair enough."

"So, you'll stay and give me a second chance?" He stood there, his hand still resting lightly on her shoulder, each slight twitch of his fingers triggering a new wave of heat through her body.

"For now at least." She didn't want to move, to step away from his touch, but if they were going to get any work done then there was no other choice. "So, did you want me to sit back down or were we planning on holding the rest of our discussion standing by the door?"

"Well, I hope you will give me a chance to apologize for my behavior, say over dinner tonight?"

Dinner?

Her? Him? Them?

Sue opened her mouth to reply only to clamp her lips tightly shut. How could she possibly go out with him?

Except it was just an apology wasn't it? And maybe a chance to go over some of the details about the blogger ring? And it wasn't exactly as if he was asking her out on a date. No, that would have been silly, a man like him could have any woman he wanted so the last person he'd be interested in was a woman like her.

"Well, do I have to beg for you to join me tonight?"

She glanced over at Barb, searching for some clue as to what she should do, but all her friend did was smile.

"All right, I'll join you for dinner then."

"Good, then I'll need your address and phone number, and I believe I'll be able to pick you up around eight, unless you have any other plans?"

Pick her up?

"She'll be ready on time, don't worry about that."

Sue shot Barb a quick look.

"Right now I'm not even sure she'll join me for dinner. Perhaps I've scared your friend off."

Oh no, he had not just gone there! "Eight will be just fine."

"Good, now we've got that part of it settled perhaps we can go back to discussing the issues raised by this blogger ring?"

"That sounds like the best idea you've had all day."

"So you stumbled across this  --  no, I'm not trying to find out how, by the way  --  and you decided to come to me with it because?"

"The other companies listed were ones I couldn't be sure about. I thought I had the abbreviations worked out but yours was the only one I could confirm." Sue took a long slow breath and met his gaze head on. Damn, why did he have to be so bloody good looking?

"We have looked into this, but with the meeting being so soon we didn't think it would be wise to delay bringing this to your attention." Barb explained.

Alan glanced over towards the other woman in the room, blinking for a moment. Had he forgotten Barb was there?

"I see, and just what do you think is behind the posts?" He turned his attention fully back on Sue.

"I think, at first, it was a way of making themselves feel like better men, getting back at women who didn't like what they saw. Or just a couple of guys being jerks over things. Then it grew into something more. I'm not entirely sure who started off the office secrets side of things, we didn't have time to dig that far into the background of the ring, but it's been going around six months." She was missing something here, a piece of the puzzle that should have been obvious but her brain refused to hand it over. "*Real Man* is the one making the posts about our building, the one in yours uses the name *Dangerous Liaisons*."

"Pranks that went too far?"

"I think so." Damnit, why hadn't she dug into matters a little more before bringing it to him? There could have been a dozen other clues in the posts on that hateful ring if she'd only taken the time to research it. "But I can give you the web address of the ring, to look into matters further."

He frowned slightly, the lines across his brow furrowing. "You're not afraid that I'll be able to work out how you tracked this ring?"

"No, I'm not. I will ask you to take things slowly though. The men behind this have done enough damage as it is."

"Oh I'm a master at taking things slowly when the need calls for it, and picking up the pace when it will get the best results for all parties involved." He grinned and looked her slowly up and down. The rest of the office fell away in that moment. Her inner walls tightened, rippled only to tighten once more. Her legs felt like Jell-O.

What was it about this man that a single look could have her wondering if he would taste good with chocolate smeared over his chest?

"I bet you are." She murmured then clamped her lips shut.

"Well now, I believe if you let me know the address then by the time we have dinner tonight I might have an idea on what we need to do next."

Yes, chocolate, all over his chest, long dark lines of sweet, sensual delight tempting her tongue down towards his cock until she could wrap her lips about it and...

"Sue? Are you all right, you just look a little distracted."

"Yes, I'm fine. Tonight it is then." She reached into a pocked in the side of her skirt, trying to force the images of Alan splayed out over his desk begging her to lick him clean, out of her mind. Maybe she'd been reading too many of those dark, erotic novels?

"You'll need this."

"Thank you." Alan reached out, stroking his fingers over hers as he claimed the paper. "And I look forward to tonight."

She shivered, her breath threatening to catch in the back of her throat as she found her gaze held and locked by a set of impossibly dark eyes. "As am I."

Yes, chocolate, whipped cream, with Alan naked and chained to a bed all eager, hungry for her touch. God, what was she thinking!

That he was the best looking man she'd seen in a long time, and even though she knew that the flirting, the soft touches and that oh-so-wicked smile he kept flashing her way were nothing more than a game it didn't stop her from enjoying it whilst she still could.

# *Chapter Six*

Alan stared at the door after the two women had left. Had he really just asked her out? From the moment she'd walked into the room he'd had to struggle to keep things on at least a semiprofessional level. Her walk, her smile, the confidence that had shone from her eyes, and yet something else, a hint of wariness when she thought he wasn't looking.

Had she been caught off guard by his invitation?

Well if she hadn't been, he had. The words had sprung to life before he'd even had the chance to think the idea through clearly.

*Just as well, if I'd thought about it then I'd have never asked her out. Shit, I'm almost ready to call her and beg out. What if she laughs at me tonight? Or backs out on her own?*

Damnit, he'd asked dozens of women out before, so why did this date, this one date, leave him feeling like a schoolboy facing his very first date all over again?

*Because I want it to work out.*

Sue. He'd never met a woman like her before now.

Just the thought of her curves, the way her smile lit up her face, the glint in her deep blue eyes when she'd stood up to him, as if she was prepared to leave him and the office if he tried to force the situation any further.

Strong.

Beautiful.

A woman, a goddess.

One capable of driving him to his knees if he let her get too close.

All right, maybe the goddess part was going a little too far, but it didn't stop his cock from throbbing at the very thought of her.

The phone rang on his desk, without the yellow light that said it had come through via reception. He frowned as he reached for the receiver; only a handful of people had the direct number.

"Hello, Alan Martin."

"Alan, it's your dad."

"Hey there." Tension eased from his shoulders as he perched on the edge of the desk. "What's up?"

"You're not going to believe this, but I had a near hysterical call from Victoria early this morning. Did something happen between the two of you? She swears that you're gay. And she's threatening to cause problems at the next social event she attends with your mother."

Alan almost slipped off the edge of the desk. "Shit, I never thought she'd go that far."

"You knew about this?"

"She's trying to get some measure of revenge, Dad. I'm not gay. In fact, I've got a date tonight with a very attractive woman. Victoria's just pissed at me."

"Revenge for what? Did you two get into a fight? She's a strong-willed woman, Alan. I would have thought you'd have learned that much about her in the time you two have been going out."

"Dad, I wouldn't call the occasional coffee and Victoria calling me three times a day our 'going out'."

"So are you going to tell me just what has her so upset?"

Great, why couldn't his dad focus on the good side of the conversation, like the date? "She's upset because I wouldn't have sex with her."

"Because you -- hold on. Did you just say you had a date for tonight?"

"Yes." Good, now he was catching on. Just as well. For one terrible moment he'd thought he might have to go back over the entire situation with Victoria. "I have a date tonight with a lovely woman I met today. I'm picking her up around eight. If everything works out, then I'd like to bring her to the party on Friday."

Would she go with him? Maybe not, but at least he could ask, if it all worked out between them.

"Is she someone I know?"

"No, Dad. No one you know. At least I don't think she is. Oh, something did come up as well; we have a lead on the people who might be behind the problems we've been dealing with of late. I'm going to look into it further, but I think we might be on to something here."

"All right, I leave that in your capable hands. But tell me how the date goes, please? I'm not trying to interfere son, I just want to see you happy."

"Sure Dad. Catch up with you later. I have a few things I need to take care of before I head out tonight."

"Okay, just let me know how it goes tomorrow morning."

Alan smiled and settled the receiver back down on the cradle. At least his day had ended with some good news. Now if only he could find out a little more about that damn blogger ring before things grew completely out of hand.

He glanced back at the work that had piled up on his desk before he reached for the phone a second time. He had a meeting to reschedule, a warning to send down to the main desk in case Victoria decided to try a new stunt, and a dinner date to arrange.

When was the last time he'd actually been out on a date, a real one? Not one pushed onto him by his father?

That was something he'd never understand. His dad, a man who backed down to his mother all the time, then pushed and shoved his way into his son's life. Was he trying to regain some level of control?

Alan sat there, the phone in one hand, his mind racing. What if his parents had the type of relationship he'd started to look for himself? One where his mum was in charge? The thought should have left him feeling uncomfortable, but the more he mused over the idea, the more it made sense. He'd not seen any overt signs of it, growing up. No whips, chains, or paddles, but there had always been that odd power dynamic between them. The way his mum only had to look at his dad to end a conversation...

He'd always known she was a strong woman, but just how far did it go?

Did they take it into the bedroom?

Alan shuddered, no matter how open minded he was, the one thing he didn't need to think about was just what his parents got up to behind closed doors.

* * * * * *

"Mr. Martin?" Steph pushed open the door to the office and peered around the edge. "Charlie needs to talk with you before you call it a night."

Charlie. He didn't need to deal with the man again today. "Does he know what time it is?"

"Yes, Mr. Martin. But he's quite insistent." She glanced behind her then shot a quick look at Alan, rolling her eyes as she gave a subtle jerk of her head. Okay, so Charlie was in hearing range, making it harder for Steph to blow him off, or give Alan a real head's up as to what was going on.

"Fine, let him in, but make sure he understands I only have about ten minutes before I need to leave for the day." He could have pushed it a little further, but he wanted plenty of time to prepare for his date with Sue. He'd already managed to get everything in place for the meeting the following morning, and only those attending the meeting now knew about the change of time and location.

"Thank you, Alan. Appreciate this."

His jaw clenched as Charlie spoke. "What can I do for you?"

"It's about the report. I need the new password to access some of the files. You changed it and..."

"And if you had everything in place you'd already have that information. Charlie, I'm growing very tired of this. Apart from that, everything you need should be in your memos and files on your own computer, unless you're claiming you never saved it, or backed up your work, which is a part of your contract if you recall?" Alan kept his voice calm as he leaned back in his chair.

Charlie paled. "No, I have everything backed up. It's just it would be easier if I could..."

"No. I changed the password for a reason and only key members of staff will be granted access. We've had far too many leaks in the past few weeks and I'm putting a stop to it."

"But, Alan, surely you don't think that I'd be involved in passing on information, do you?" Charlie took a step closer to the desk. "And I need that access. I can't do my job properly without it."

"Charlie Welch, you haven't been doing your job properly to begin with. Your reports are always late, you've had more hard drive crashes, email errors, and file corruption issues than the rest of this company put together."

"I've been unlucky, and I think I've pissed off a few people in the company so they're..."

"Out to get you?" Alan's jaw tightened.

"Yes, sure."

Did the man not understand how foolish he sounded? Did he really believe that his story was plausible? "Charlie, I'm going to make this very clear to you. You will get this report done, using the files on your computer, the copies you told me you'd made when I first spoke to you about this. Now if there had really been an issue you'd have brought it up to me this morning and shown me the proof. So it sounds to me as though you're stalling for time."

"It's not like that."

"Then you won't object to my taking a look at your computer tomorrow, or rather having our tech department do it, will you?"

Charlie shook his head. "That won't be needed, sir. I've got everything I need. I just thought it would be best to double-check some of the files. I'm sorry I bothered you about this. I know you're pressed for time."

Alan didn't bother to hide his smile. "You know where the door is, Charlie."

"Yes sir, again, my apologies." The man darted out of the office before Alan had a chance to say anything else.

Alan watched the door close, the soft click ringing through the room, his gaze narrowing. Just what was that man up to? Why would he come in to try and get the password when he had to know just how much trouble he was in? He wasn't the first employee to try and get the new password, and no doubt wouldn't be the last, but why take the risk when he knew he was on thin ice to begin with?

The intercom beeped on his desk.

"Yes?"

"You asked me to remind you of your appointment tonight, and now that Charlie's gone…" Steph's voice rang out through the unit on his desk.

"Thank you, I'll be heading out shortly." He had better things to spend his time on than wondering about Charlie Welch and his never-ending supply of excuses.

At least he'd be able to end the day on a pleasant note …

# *Chapter Seven*

"I can't believe you stood up to him like that." Barb pulled a brush through Sue's hair. "I've never seen you like that before, but I have to say that I like this new side of your nature."

"I was shaking like a leaf the entire time." Sue admitted and tried not to wince. "I'm not sure how I managed to talk back to him, it didn't help that I kept thinking he was flirting with me. It had to be a case of the nerves, though, I'm just not his taste. Besides, he needed putting back in his place and he just asked me out to get back at me for that."

"Are you nuts? He was flirting with you the entire time. I could have been invisible for the most part through that entire meeting. Why would he ask you out for revenge?"

"Then he was just trying to put me at ease, or else being polite." Sue tried to shrug it off. "I don't know what he's up to, but whatever it is I'm betting he's not just after a simple date. I don't trust him. He's got dozens of women he could have asked out, why me unless it's a game, a way of lashing out at me?"

"Right, and I'm a multimillionaire. Sue, he was really flirting with you. He liked you. God knows I've seen enough men flirt with women before now to know when they are hitting on someone, and when they are just trying to pass the time, or use it to distract someone. No, he really did like you. You should have seen the way his eyes lit up when you walked back to the chair. He couldn't look away from your ass."

"You're nuts. There's no way a man who looks like that would have any interest in me! He could have any woman he wanted, why in hell's name would he want me?"

"Yeah, then why did he ask to meet you for dinner tonight? Sue, sometimes you completely miss the obvious. And no, he's not taking you for a meal just to try and find some weird way to humiliate you."

"All right, then fine. He's asked me out to discuss this whole blogger thing of course, why else would he ask me out?" So why did her heart skip a beat at the thought of meeting him again.

Sue closed her eyes, trying to find a way to calm down, but all she could think of was Alan on his knees at her feet. She could almost feel it, his lips caressing her feet, her legs, touching her, tempting her senses until she shivered and focused on Barb's words instead.

"If it was business, or just that, he wouldn't have invited you to join him for a meal at one of the best restaurants in town." Barb slapped her on the arm with the back of the brush. "Stop kidding yourself. He's interested in you."

"Ow!" Sue hissed and rubbed the stinging red mark. "Bitch! That hurt."

"It was meant to. Now sit still and let me finish your hair."

Sue grumbled but tried to get her nerves, and body, back under control. "So, why do you think he invited me for dinner then, if it wasn't to discuss business?"

"Try something simple, such as he likes you." Barb chuckled and pulled the brush slowly through Sue's hair.

"No, men don't like women like me."

"Oh hush now. You're an attractive woman. I don't care what Bill, or other idiots like him say. Now just take a deep breath and calm down. He'll be here in a bit and we really need to get you all spruced up for him."

Sue sucked in her bottom lip and tried not to look into the mirror. "I'm just not sure about all of this."

"If you can't trust yourself then at least trust me. He might come off as a bit of an arrogant jerk, but you stood up to him and I think he liked that. Once he'd stopped choking."

"Oh God, I don't know how I managed to stand up to him like that. I thought for certain we were fucked at that point."

"Well whatever was going through your mind, it worked. And you impressed him. I don't think a woman's managed to do that in a long time."

That part she couldn't argue with. "You know much about him?"

"Not a huge amount, but I did a little asking around after our meeting. Seems Alan has a decent reputation with women, but doesn't date in house, not that I could find. Keeps a separation between his work and his social life."

"All right, that sounds good. Not everyone is like that." How many men and women had she known through the years that took advantage of any scrap of power they had? Too many were far too willing to use it in order to get their own way. "So you think he's a good man?"

"I think he might be and I don't see any harm in having one night out with him. A good dinner might be just what you need to cheer you up. An evening out on the town with a man like that on your arm -- well I have to admit that if you weren't my best friend I'd make a play for him myself."

It didn't stop the doubts though.

"So why didn't you? Come on, we both know how good looking he is. And he has money. Position. Shit, a man like that would look good on the cover of a magazine."

"Friends don't play games like that with each other. Besides, even if we weren't friends it was very clear, from the moment we walked into his office, that the only one he was interested in was you." Barb set the brush down and leaned forward, wrapping her arms about Sue. "You need to start believing in yourself, love. Today, yesterday, both times you let the real you come out. The strength I've seen in you each and every day since we first met. But you let it out fully the past few days."

"That was different. Bill had it coming. And Alan, well I wasn't in the mood to deal with anyone trying to tell me what to do." Sue glanced in the mirror. The woman looking back at her barely seemed familiar. Soft curls of golden brown hair hung in loose waves around her face. Her lips had been painted with a delicate pale pink hue, just enough to bring them to life. Each touch of makeup had been gentle, a hint, little more than a way of bringing attention to her face, to the full sensual lips she had never known she possessed.

"You look beautiful."

How could she argue that, now that she could see the final results of her best friend's hard work.

"Do you think he'll be pleased?"

"The question is, are you pleased with how you look? Who cares what he thinks? I didn't do this for him you know."

"I'm trying to look at it that way, really I am but..."

"But you've not been out on a date in a long time and you're worried he won't like what he sees." Barb gave a quick squeeze and settled down on the chair nearby. "I can't tell you if he will like how you look, but I can tell you he certainly enjoyed watching you earlier today."

It didn't settle her nerves.

Find an image that would help, that's all she had to do. And one came back to her all too easily. She squirmed on the chair, her thighs pressed tightly together as she tried not to let the wicked thoughts take control of her mind.

Just the thought of him with those trails of dark, sweet, sticky chocolate smeared across his body triggered a wave of heat through her core. Would he ask her to lick it off, or keep her at arm's length until she -- no he'd beg for her touch, after all it was her dream and she could set it in any way she wanted.

"Do you think he likes chocolate?"

"What?" Barb shot her a hard look.

"Oh, nothing. Just some silly thoughts I kept having earlier today, whilst we were in his office." Silly, delicious thoughts that had warmed her heart -- and other parts of her anatomy -- but Sue was all too well aware that sometimes a fantasy needed to stay as just that.

"Share. Come on, we don't keep secrets from each other. I'm not about to let you start now."

Heat flashed across her face as she shifted on the chair. "You'll laugh at me."

"Maybe I'll laugh with you?"

There was always that possibility. "I kept thinking about him sprawled over his desk, his chest covered in chocolate as he begged me to touch him."

"Oh God, you didn't go there! Sue!"

Sue felt her cheeks turn scarlet instantly. "Well, yes. But only in my thoughts. It's not as if I actually said something to him about that."

"Now I thought I was being bad. I kept having images of him on his knees licking his way up my legs."

"Barb!"

"Well he is cute."

She couldn't argue with that one. "Do you think he has a girl-friend?"

"No, if he did then he wouldn't have asked you out."

Sue glanced up at the clock. "I don't know if he's really going to turn up. What if this is all part of some nasty joke, or he's a member of the blogger ring and this is a way of smearing my name all over that nasty circle?"

Barb shook her head. "No, that doesn't make sense and you know it. If he was a part of that ring, then he'd stay well away from you. They really don't have any time for women with any form of strength and that turned him on. Big time. The men on that ring are obnoxious control freaks who wouldn't know what to do with a strong woman if their lives depended on it."

It didn't silence the doubts though.

"He'll be here soon."

"I know." *If he ever turned up at all. I mean, no matter what Barb says, he's still a young, handsome, rich guy who doesn't need a woman like me in his life.*

A loud chime drew her attention away from the mirror.

Barb hurried away to the window. "He's here. Nice car too. BMW I think, can't really tell from up here."

"I can't do this."

"Yes, you can." Barb hurried out into the living room, towards the front door.

Sue swallowed hard and tried to force her stomach into some semblance of normal behavior. This wasn't a good idea. She'd make a fool of herself. He'd try to force her into a situation she wouldn't be able to handle...

Did she have time to back out of this?

No, it was already far too late for that.

"Is Sue ready?" Alan's voice carried back into the bedroom. "I don't think I'm too early."

"Yes, she is. Please, sit down. I'll let her know you're here."

Sue glanced back around the room, pity there wasn't somewhere she could hide.

"Sue?" Barb peeked around the corner. "Come on, it's time. He's ready for you."

A date, a real date after all those years of waiting for someone to take notice of her. Wasn't this what she had been waiting for? So why did she feel as though she was heading out for an execution?

Still, he had come to pick her up, and he was real, and good looking, so it wasn't as though she'd been lied to about that. This wasn't a bad blind date set up out of pity by someone else. She'd been through more than one of those, and had no intention of being dragged into any more.

"Are you going to keep him waiting?"

"No, I guess not." Better to get it over and done with. Sue pushed to her feet and almost sat back down again instantly as her legs threatened to give out from beneath her. The butterflies in her stomach turned into snakes that wrapped themselves around each other and threatened to turn her guts inside out. "Oh, God. I just can't do this."

"Don't be silly. He's waiting out there for you right now." Barb folded her arms beneath her breasts, her voice little more than a whisper. "Now either get out there or I'll drag you out."

"You wouldn't!"

"Do you really want to try me on that?"

No, she didn't. Sue took a deep breath, wrestled the snakes under control and stood up. "All right then, let's get this over and done with."

"Stop trying to look at this as if you're being sent to your own funeral. It really isn't that bad."

There spoke a woman who had never been through the agony of a date that had gone wrong from start to finish.

Barb pushed open the door and led the way back out into the living room.

A low wolf whistle made her look up.

"Damn, you look good." Alan murmured. "I knew I was lucky when you agreed to go out with me earlier today, but I didn't realize just how far that run of good luck went."

Sue opened her mouth to speak then shut it again quickly. Was he joking? Pulling a fast one on her? She fixed a hard look on him, searching for some sign, a hint that this was nothing more than a cruel joke.

A soft smile graced his lips, a warmth danced within his eyes. He hadn't taken a seat but stood close to the door dressed in a black shirt, pants, and jacket with a scarlet tie. He'd put a tie on for her? Had he worn one in the office as well? Not that she could recall. Damn, he'd pushed out all the stops for her and for what? So he could embarrass her in some way? No, Barb was right, that didn't make any sense at all.

"So, are you ready to join me for dinner, Sue?" He gave a low, swooping bow, an elegant gesture of a bygone age, and offered her his left hand.

She glanced over at Barb, who nodded quickly, jerking her head towards the door. All right already, she got the hint. Even if it had taken her most of the day to accept that her best friend was right.

"Yes, I think I am."

"Then shall we?"

# *Chapter Eight*

"So, what made you agree to come out with me?" Alan leaned back in the chair and cupped a glass of wine in one hand. "I saw the look in your eyes when I first asked you out, you didn't think I was serious."

Sue waited for a moment as a waiter came and cleared away her now empty plate. For once she hadn't felt as if every mouthful had been judged. Instead Alan had done the exact opposite, he'd steered the conversation to light, easy topics, ranging from music to current affairs. The past two hours had been calm and relaxing until the last of her inner doubts had finally crawled back under their rock and left her to enjoy the evening with him.

"I'm not sure why I said yes."

"Yet you did anyway? That shows a lot of courage. Especially after reading through some of the entries on that blogger ring. I believe I managed to identify which blogger refers to some of the women in the company. And if that man, *Real Man,* I believe that was his online name, is one you have to deal with on a daily basis then I admire your courage. I've already started to look into that ring, but I'm afraid we might have to seek help from the police before we will be able to take it very far."

Courage? If she had been so courageous then why had she spent all that time shaking like a leaf, trying to find a reason, any reason, not to join him for dinner? And bringing the police in on the entire blogger ring opened up another potential problem for Ann or rather her brother. That was something she'd need to discuss with the woman as soon as possible.

Or at least first thing in the morning.

"So why did you ask me out then? There must be a dozen women you see on a daily basis who would love to share an evening with you?"

## Curvaeous Heart

"Maybe there are, but part of a date is being able to enjoy the time with that person and I -- well, I like you." Alan shifted in his seat, twin points of color touching his cheeks. "I know that you think I must be the sort of man who goes out with -- well, I'm not sure what you think of me. But I knew when you walked into my office that there was something special about you. The way you stood up to me, no one's ever done that to me before, not at work at least. Even Dad gives into me on most things."

Now that did surprise her. Mr. Martin Senior was well known to be a strong-willed and determined man who had brought the company up from almost nothing at all. "I bet you still manage to go head to head at times."

"On rare occasions, but he's pretty much taken a step back from things recently. Especially with some of the deals we currently have on the table. So to find someone willing to damn near shout me down in my own office caught me off guard. In a pleasant way, of course."

"I'm surprised you didn't have us kicked out of your office. I would have lost my temper and had you removed if the roles had been reversed."

Alan set the glass down and leaned forward, reaching out across the table to stroke his fingers over her hand. "Now why would I do that when all I wanted to do in that moment was pull you over the edge of my desk and explore every inch of your body with my tongue?"

It took a moment before she realized what he'd said. Heat flushed across her cheeks, her breath caught in the back of her throat as she fought to keep control and to prevent her sudden urge to crawl under the table to hide.

"Ah, not the sort of thing you were expecting to hear?" Alan's full lips twitched in a flicker of disappointment before a smooth smile returned to mask his emotions. "Perhaps I'm not the sort of man you'd find attractive. I can understand that, I did come across as a complete and utter arrogant asshole."

"No, it's not that." Not find him attractive? Was he nuts? He had to be one of the most gorgeous men she had ever seen.

"Then?"

"I wasn't expecting to hear that from you." Nor from any man, if she was going to be brutally honest. Not unless it was part of a cruel practical joke and she'd been the brunt of those for far too many years.

"Why not? You're attractive, strong willed, intelligent with more than a hint of courage. You're the sort of woman that any man in their right mind would give their soul to spend time with."

"Most people don't think that way about women like me." She looked away from him, trying to force her thoughts into some semblance of order. "I mean I'm not exactly a size 5 here. And I'm past my sell by date."

"And why would that matter?"

Sue turned back to look at him. "Well, don't most men want something slim and young?"

"Funny, you look like you have all your teeth to me and honestly speaking, if I wanted a stick insect that would break the first time we tried to play then I'd spend my time hanging around models. Sorry, but that type really doesn't appeal to me. Most of the ones I've met in the past couple of years have been *me, me, me, and oh yeah, me.*"

He hadn't moved his hand and as he spoke he stroked her fingers gently with his own. Each light touch sent a wave of shivering delight through her body. Heat rippled through her inner walls, a need throbbed along her labia into her clit until she was left wondering just what he would feel like buried deep within her vulva.

"Are they all like that?"

"No, there are some good ones out there. Just, well they don't appeal to me. Not as lovers, or anything more than friends. I'd break them if I tried to do anything with them. I mean I'm not a weak man. I work out most days, and if I tried to thrust into a woman who barely weighed more than my office bag on a good day,

### *Curvaeous Heart*

I'd leave them bruised or with broken bones. That's not what I call attractive."

"You have to have seen the pictures, the news reports, those skinny models walking up and down the catwalk. That's what men find attractive, not women like me."

"Did you know that up until around the turn of the nineteenth century women who were that thin were looked on as being sick? Just look at the artwork of the time period. The women there, the nudes, are Rubenesque. They didn't paint thin women; they didn't find them attractive. The women in those paintings had hips, curves, and breasts. They had the figure of a woman, with all the wonderful, soft skin and padding in between."

"So maybe I was born in the wrong era?" Sue almost smiled.

"Or men, and the fashion industry, need to remember just why we need women with a little meat on their bones. You've no idea how badly I wanted to strip you down in the middle of my office and explore you. I thought you'd turn me down about dinner and now, sitting here, sharing dinner with you, I've kept wondering what you look like under that wonderful dress. I want a real woman, not a woman with the body of a boy whose bones are going to jab into me at precisely the wrong moment."

A soft giggle threatened to gain life and Sue swallowed hard, forcing it back into submission. "I hadn't really looked at it that way before. I just thought men like that type of woman."

"Don't get me wrong, some do. But they're not for me." He traced the tips of his fingers along the back of her hand, leaving shivering circular patterns across her flesh. "So I have to ask, would you consider more than just a single dinner date with me?"

"You mean a second date?"

"And a third, fourth, fifth, however many you'd be willing to en-joy with me"

"And if I wanted more than just dinner with you? Say something a little more intimate? Perhaps involving chocolate?" God, where had that come from! She wasn't like this normally.

Alan's lips parted softly, the tip of his tongue snaking out from between them. A merry light shone within his eyes as a devilish smile triggered a set of dimples in his cheeks.

"I'm sorry, shit, I don't know why I -- I didn't mean to say that. Please ignore..."

"Sue, nothing would please me more than to spend that time with you." He reached out with his free hand and cupped her chin, lifting it up until she had no choice but to look him directly in the eyes. "I don't want to push you into anything though. Yes I want you, more than I should considering we only just met, but unfortunately my body doesn't particularly care about time. However, my mind, my heart, they both want you to be happy and ready to make that step with me."

Was she dreaming?

Men like this didn't really exist. They just wanted sex, there and then and to hell with what a woman wanted. Her jaw tightened as she watched his face.

"Did I say something wrong?"

"No, it's just that I'm not used to a man acting the way you do. I barely know what to think. First you tell me that I'm the body type you prefer, now when I offer you the chance to get laid you tell me you're willing to wait until I'm certain it's the right step for me? Do you know how rare that is?"

"I've got a fair idea, yes." Alan nodded and leaned back in the chair, bringing his hands to rest on the table. "I've been around enough men my age who focus on getting laid, with as many women as they can. That blogger reminded me just how many men out there treat women as little more than playthings, but I'm not like that and never have been."

Sue took a long hard look back at Alan. The shape of his jaw, the way the muscles played beneath his shirt. Even the soft curl of black hair that now teased into the middle of his forehead.

He really wanted her.

No joke, no hidden agenda, no harsh words. He was just a man who looked at her with an undeniable heat in his gaze and a hunger in his smile.

"And if I don't want to wait?"

"I wouldn't be a gentleman if I didn't let the lady set the pace, would I? And I was raised to be every inch the gentleman when it came to such matters."

*And if I don't want you to be a gentleman? If I want you to strip me off, kiss every part of my body, and then make me scream your name, what then?*

She sucked in her bottom lip. No. She couldn't say that to him either. Even if she wanted to. But she had to say something to him, leaving him hanging wouldn't do either of them any good and she needed him. No, wanted him. If she was going to be that honest about the situation it was a want, a sweet, delicious want, but not a need.

He wasn't the type of man who would force her, he'd stop if she wanted him to, so she was safe with him.

"Then, if you're serious, I believe I'd like to extend our evening together."

* * * * * *

"So who is it that has you so nervous around me?" Alan glanced over at her as he slipped the key into the ignition. "I wasn't aware that I'd done anything to spook you."

"I -- I'm not sure what you mean."

"Yes, you are, Sue." He leaned back in the seat and twisted just enough to meet her gaze fully. "I can see it in your eyes. I know you want this and that you want to be out with me, to go home with me if only for a couple of hours, but I can also see something else in you. A slight flinch, the way you listen very carefully to anything I say as if you're looking for the hidden knife in the words. It's not an ex-boyfriend thing either. So who it is?"

Sue chewed slowly on the inside of her lip, twisting her hands in her lap.

"You don't have to tell me if you don't want to, but I'd really like to know." Did she think he would use the information against her? Well depending on what sort of men she'd spent time with then yes, she might well believe that. "You're a strong woman, Sue. Whoever it is only has power over you if you let them have it. I think you know that."

"That sounds all well and good, but if you go to work every day and hear the same jokes, the snide comments, the jabs and *wide load* remarks then you'd think differently."

Work, all right, so not an ex-boyfriend. Good. "And your work hasn't done anything about him?"

"They never catch him. Bloody asshole knows not to try anything like that around witnesses, or most of the time at least."

"Ah, he makes mistakes on occasions?"

"Bill did today."

At least he now had a name to go by. "And what did Bill do today?"

"He tried something in the corridor by the copy room and someone overheard him. He didn't know, nor did I, but I stood up to him for the first time since he started picking on me. He has something against women of my build."

"Or he's attracted to you and too scared to say anything."

She chuckled and ducked her head a little. "Well he does try and cop a feel every chance he gets, but he tends to be more interested in the skinny young things. Goes through them quickly though. I'm honestly surprised he hasn't been fired yet, but I guess most of them are too ashamed to file a complaint."

Now that part he could understand in a roundabout way. He'd seen more than one newcomer to the company bluster their way out of filing a report about sexual harassment in case it backfired on them. Or because it boiled down to he said, she said. Unless there was a witness to some, if not all, of the problems that the man or men had caused.

### *Curvaeous Heart*

"So what are you going to do about him?" Alan turned the key fully and started up the car. "Or are you going to keep on letting him make women unhappy?"

"Not much I can do, unless he pulls some more shit around me. I've stood up to him once, so I can do it again, but only if I catch him at it. And that's the hard part." She sighed and brushed a stray lock of hair back from her eyes.

His gaze wandered for a brief moment, lingering on her legs until he reminded himself he should be concentrating on his driving instead of how good his passenger looked.

"Well, I just hope someone catches him out soon, other than you I mean."

"I think he might have pushed things a little too far recently." Sue murmured. "In more ways than one -- God I am so tired of his constant snide remarks. The fatty comments, the elbow in the side, pressing me up against the wall to try and grab a feel when he walks past, but he's done worse things than that to other people. I ..." She looked away.

"Is there something wrong?"

"Nothing, no. I just don't want to ruin the evening by talking about him anymore tonight. He's ruined enough things for me in the past couple of months, last thing I need is the spirit of Bill in the middle of our evening."

What else had gone on between them?

Not something he could really press about right now, no matter how much he wanted to. The frown that creased her brow, the way her hands tangled into the skirt of her dress and that slight hitch in her voice when she had been talking about him.

No, she was right about one thing. This Bill, whoever he was, had taken enough time from her life as it was, and didn't deserve a place in what remained of their evening together.

## *Chapter Nine*

His house. She'd agreed to go to his house. Without calling Barb to let her know what was going on? This wasn't sane. Shit, what had gotten into her?

*With any luck a stud called Alan.*

"Are you sure you want to do this?" Alan led her into the living room. "I don't want to push you into something."

"Have you changed your mind?" Her heart threatened to drop down through her stomach. She'd come this far, if he backed out... Oh shit, what if the entire evening, the meal, the invitation, even bringing her to his home, had all just been a way of embarrassing her?

No, she hadn't picked up that type of vibe from him.

"I haven't. I guess I just wasn't expecting you to want this, not so soon." Alan smiled, walked across the room and turned down the lights. A soft glow lit the room now, a large leather couch sat in front of an open fireplace. Behind that, through a set of double doors, she could see what had to be a king-size bed. He glanced back at her before pressing a small button to one side of the fire-place. With a crack a tiny flame danced across the prepared kindling and within moments a small fire had embraced the thin strips of wood. A real fire, she hadn't been expecting that, but it was a nice touch. She'd only heard of a few people who still used them, most had switched over to natural gas years ago. All that was missing was a traditional thick rug; still, the couch and the bed she had caught a glimpse of would work just as well. "I'm not complaining. It's a little like planning on climbing a mountain in five stages, only to find you reach the top on the first day."

"Are -- did you just compare me to a mountain?" Her jaw clenched.

"No, not like that. I meant as in the way of a challenge. Shit,

### *Curvaeous Heart*

I didn't exactly phrase that the right way did I?" He looked back at her, flushed as he built up the fire before closing the protective glass back over the fireplace. "I'm sorry."

"Not really." Well that was one thing, he didn't have that fully confident, everything's going my way type of attitude. "But we all make mistakes."

"Thanks. Do you want a drink? I can get you a brandy, or martini?" Alan kicked off his shoes and leaned over a small cabinet, tapping the bottles on what looked like a circular, silver tray. She watched him carefully as he moved, the way his pants tightened over his ass. Her fingers itched with a growing need to strip the clothing from his body. It would have been so easy to walk up behind him and trace her fingers over the taut curves of his sweet buttocks.

Did he know just how intently she was watching him? Or that she had spent the best part of the day, when she hadn't been fighting against the urge to curl in a corner, thinking about him? About the way his body moved, the light that played in his eyes, his smile and those full, sensual lips how they would feel pressed against hers?

"So did you want something to drink?"

"No, I'm doing fine, thanks." No she didn't need a drink, she needed him. She wanted him more than she'd ever known could be possible. His shirt half slipped free from the back of his pants, baring just a flash of skin, a hint of the man beneath the cloth. It wouldn't have taken much to reach out and pull the shirt the rest of the way out of his pants. "What I need isn't a drink."

Alan turned back to look at her. "And what is it you want?"

"You." A week ago, even a day, she wouldn't have had the nerve to tell him that, but something had changed. Seeing Bill all but run down the corridor, finally discovering what type of man he was, and that she wasn't afraid of him anymore, had changed a few things within her.

"So what are you going to do about that?"

"I wasn't sure at first, but I have a vague idea forming in the back of my mind." She felt a hungry smile tug at her lips. Did she have the guts to go through with this?

Yes.

Sue took a slow breath and tried to calm her nerves. She wanted him, that much was certain. All the way through dinner she'd wondered what it would be like to feel his body against hers.

"And what do you want me to do?"

She smiled, an image forming in her mind. What if he really meant what he said? She could finally explore what it would be like to take charge, to have a man follow through with her every whim and desire. Would he do that, would he risk that?

Well, why not?

There was only one way to find out.

"I want you to stand there and let me take control of everything."

"Oh you think I'm going to do that?" One dark eyebrow vanished beneath the wave of black hair.

"You said you liked strong women. So why not prove it, show me just how much you like that in a woman. Put your money where your mouth is." Her heart pounded against her chest. It would have been so easy for the mood to vanish and she could find herself escorted out of his home for trying to push things too far.

"Ah, a challenge."

"Yes, do you think you're up to it?" God, she hoped so.

For a moment he didn't move, the light from the fireplace caressed his form, casting shadows about the room.

"Yes, I believe so, but there's only one way to find out, isn't there?" The other men? He could see that written across her face? All the mistakes, the problems she'd walked headlong into, he could tell that she'd been through all of that? How?

"I'm not like them, Sue. All I'm doing is asking you to trust me."

Sue nodded and cleared the distance between them, slipping out of her shoes as she walked across the room. She sucked in her bottom lip, hissing gently as she reached out for him, tracing her fingers over his chest. He trembled beneath her touch, but didn't move away from her.

"You like that?"

Alan nodded, shaking a little.

"And if I wanted to do more?"

"There's only one way to find out, isn't there?" He winked and crossed his hands behind his back. "It's not going to be easy, to let you take control of the situation, but I can at least try."

"And if you don't manage it, maybe I'll have to find a way to punish you." Now where had that come from? She'd thought, briefly, about Bill being on his knees at the feet of a dominatrix. Then there had been the whole image of Alan covered in chocolate and begging to be licked clean, but this  --  no this was taking that little game to a whole new level.

"Punish me?" A slight tremble ran through his body.

"Well that's what happens to boys who don't do as their told."

He growled. "The last thing I am is a boy."

"Ah now, that we will just have to wait and see about, if you can keep still long enough." Sue tugged at his shirt, pulling the last of it out of his pants. "If you can do as you're told then I'll find a way to reward you."

"Now that sounds more like it." He flashed a wicked grin. "Though I suppose I could submit to a punishment if the need arose."

Clean, taut skin tempted her fingers as she unbuttoned the shirt and pushed it back from his shoulders. With his hands crossed behind his back it caught on his wrists. With a slight shrug he uncrossed his hands long enough to let the shirt fall to the floor before returning them to his self-imposed position.

She leaned in close, inhaling. Spices, sweet musk and spices. Flawless skin, at least what she could see so far matched that description. Would the rest of him be as perfect? What had she done to find a man like this? Had she won the lottery? Or just stumbled on a piece of good luck?

*No, shut that thought down right now. Deserve? Find? Shit, he wants me, the rest doesn't matter.*

He shuddered beneath her light touch, his eyes closed as he tried not to move. His cock swelled beneath his pants, pushing at the material even as she reached for his belt and slowly undid it, pulling it from the loops in a single, smooth motion.

"Are you going to do this slowly?" He murmured, his voice husky, breath catching with each word. "Tormenting me?"

"Yes, I think so." Sue leaned in, nibbling a soft path across his chest. Even his sweat tasted good. Small hairs tickled at her lips and curled about his nipples, tempting her to capture the tiny bud. "I'm going to taste you in tiny bites, licking you, nipping, suckling until you beg for me to take that a little bit further."

He groaned, shoulders tensing. "Heavenly torture, and I think you're going to enjoy every minute of it."

Torture, for both of them.

Her vulva rippled, heat coating her lower lips, her clit aching for his touch, but she'd been given the chance to set the pace and she wasn't about to surrender that, even if her body had other ideas. She ruled here, not her body, her dreams, or her fears.

Somewhere deep within, the final chains that held her secret desires locked tight finally shattered. Sue slipped her tongue out between her lips and licked a light path about one taut, pink nipple. Tiny hairs teased the tip of her nose, but she didn't care. His soft groan, the tiny shiver that rippled through his chest, and the throb of his cock against his pants, urged her on.

She eased one hand down over the growing tent of his pants, grasping his erection gently. He arched into her touch, heels leaving the floor.

"God!"

"You like that?" She stroked him softly through his pants.

"Yes!"

"You want more?" His cock throbbed against her hand.

"Yes, please, yes."

"Then you can wait." She gave him another light squeeze then released her hold.

"Witch!"

"That's one thing I haven't been called before now." She leaned up, wrapping her arms about his neck as she pulled his head down for a kiss.

"I can think of some other wicked little names to call you." He whispered against her lips. "Ones that might make that sweet little pussy of yours twitch."

"I bet you could." She nibbled softly against his lower lip, suckling it into her mouth as he groaned. He tried to lick against her upper lip only to whimper as she pulled away. "But for now, I'm more interested in doing this."

She tightened her grip on his neck and claimed his lips, sliding her tongue into the depths of his mouth. She'd never been given full control of a situation like this before and she wasn't about to miss out on the chance. Her tongue swept slowly along the confines of his mouth, tickling across the surface of his tongue before drawing his into her mouth and suckling softly on it.

Her heart beat against her rib cage, every movement, however slight that he made, left her wondering if he were about to break position and take control of the situation, but he didn't.

With a soft moan she pressed her hands against his chest and broke the kiss, stepping back from him. "Stay still."

He nodded, opening his eyes.

She reached for the zipper at the back of her dress, pulling it down slowly as his gaze locked on her. His eyes narrowed, lips parting softly as he licked over them, watching as she eased the dress down about her waist. Soft cups of black, lacey cotton lifted up her breasts, a matching pair of black lace panties covered her mound and the straps of her suspender belt held up the stockings. Thigh highs had been a bad idea the one time she'd worn them, even the ones apparently designed for larger women still rolled down her thighs at the wrong moment.

"Damn." He whispered.

"Thank you." Her cheeks burned as she lowered her gaze for a moment. "Stay right there."

He nodded, swallowing hard as he watched her every move.

She stepped out of the dress, setting it on the arm of the couch, then stood up fully and reached for the opening to her bra, her breasts pushed out as she stretched to find the clasps. His eyes widened, the tip of his tongue pushed between his lips, his cock throbbed under his pants and every breath he took caused his erection to strain against the soft cloth.

Liquid heat covered her lower lips, moistening her panties.

No man had ever made her feel this way. Not even by touching her. And yet here he was, standing there, bare-chested, and she felt almost ready to beg him to touch her, take her, make her scream in need. Instead she somehow managed to keep those needs silent, buried deeply. At least for now.

She unhooked her bra and let it drop onto the floor. With a soft shiver she traced her fingers back around her chest, cupping her breasts, lifting them up into view. Her nipples throbbed even as she closed her fingers around them. He groaned, watching her every move, hips twitching as he struggled to remain in control of his body. Did he want to move? If so, why wasn't he saying anything about it?

She moaned, sliding her fingers down from her breasts and into the sides of her panties. "Do you want to see more?"

He growled and gave a slight nod of his head. "Please."

"Maybe I should make you wait?" She traced her fingers along her hips, following the line of her panties. "I could just sit back on your couch and watch you, touching myself through my panties, waiting until you're ready to beg for more."

"Evil woman!"

"Is that a yes?"

"No!"

## *Curvaeous Heart*

Sue wriggled a little, her fingers hooked back into the sides of her panties, her eyes locked with his.

"Please, take them off."

There it was, the plea. She'd never had a man plead with her before now, not over something like this, and the thrill of power his words gave her was intoxicating.

"Ask me again."

"Please, Sue, don't keep me waiting. I want to see you. I need to see what you look like. In every glorious detail. What do I have to say?"

"I think you already know." Her breath caught in the back of her throat. "What do you call someone you've given power to?"

"Please, ma'am." He didn't even hesitate. "Ma'am, I'm begging you, please take them off."

He'd done it, he'd really done it.

She slid her panties down slowly, easing them past the straps of her suspender belt until she stepped out of them completely. Until she stood there only in her stockings and suspenders.

"I didn't know anyone still wore those, but fuck, they look good on you. A frame, a luscious, sensual frame"

A frame? She glanced down and blushed. The two straps did look like that. And she could see just what they were presenting to him. Her mound. A soft, down-covered mound.

"I don't want to wait any longer, Sue. Please, just let me touch you, kiss you, hold you."

"Have you forgotten already?" She gave a mock frown.

"Ma'am. Please."

She shook her head, not trusting herself to speak anymore as she walked back towards him and slowly dropped to her knees. Without a sound she reached up and unfastened his pants, sliding them and his brief black underpants down his thighs. She was in control here, not him, not this time at least.

Sue reached up and cupped his balls. Holding them gently. His cock throbbed, thick and erect in front of her face, the head swollen, glistening with his own need, his scent heady, calling to her, begging that she take him within her mouth, do something, anything to relieve the pressure that rocked through his body.

"Step out of your pants."

He shifted quickly, trembling beneath her fingers. "You've no idea what you're doing to me."

"Oh, I think I do." With the way her own body screamed for attention, the pressure that threatened to ripple out of control she had a damn good idea of just what he was going through.

"What are you going to do down there?"

Sue edged a little further forward on her hands and knees and opened her mouth, capturing the head of his cock between her lips. With a low groan she licked quickly across it, purring into his erection.

"Shit!" He cried out, back arching as he struggled to keep his hands locked behind his back. "Much more of that and there's no way I'll be able to keep still!"

She smiled around his cock, massaging his balls gently with one hand, her other wrapped about the base of his erection. With tiny, teasing licks, she covered the length of his member in small kisses, a touch of her tongue, suckling him into the depths of her mouth only to pull back until she only held the head of his cock in her mouth.

"I can't."

But he could, she knew he could. All it would take was the right amount of persuasion. She reached back with one finger, keeping her hand about his balls as that one finger began to massage a small, hidden spot behind his sac.

She suckled him fully into her mouth, wrapping her fingers about his cock, squeezing, releasing, only to squeeze again. She pressed her fingertip back against that sensitive spot, knowing each time she did he would groan, half plead with her, only to settle back on his heels once more and struggle to keep in position.

She could taste him, thick, heady and needful, on her tongue.

## Curvaeous Heart

Each pulse through his erection heightened her own desire. Sue lifted up away from the head of his cock and blew, very gently, over the slick, glistening skin.

"Sue, please!"

*Please what? Continue, push him back, rock on his cock until he came and came and came, trapped in between her tight, eager walls? Such a very tempting image.*

"You want me?"

"Yes."

"And if I wanted to leave now, end it, change my mind and not follow things through."

He groaned and closed his eyes, shivering. "I'd let you go. The choice is yours. It's always been yours."

Would he really go that far, let her walk out of the door when every inch of his body craved her touch? She watched him, searching his face for some hint that he was lying, trying to lead her on, but she could still hear his words, that plea he had made earlier for her to trust him.

*I've come this far, he's not hurt me yet, not made any moves that would cross the line. If I'm prepared to play the game, then I better see it through to the end. Besides, I want it just as much as he does.*

"I think we'll take this to the bedroom then."

# *Chapter Ten*

Alan held out his hand to her. "Walk with me."

She nodded, tangling her fingers with his. The years between them no longer mattered in this moment. He wanted her, needed her in his life, even if it was just for one night.

She'd even sensed what he needed, truly needed in a woman. Did he know that she'd never taken that step with someone else? Demanded they obey her, call her ma'am? Had he spent all those years of searching for a woman with the strength to put him too his knees only to find she'd been working for him...

Silently, dressed only in her suspender belt and stockings, she walked with him into the bedroom. Even if he turned his back on her, left her the same way others had, it wouldn't matter. At least she would be able to enjoy tonight, on her terms.

Soft pillows and a thick comforter decorated the bed. Two lamps, one on either side of the bed -- a large, old fashioned piece of furniture that wouldn't have been easy to find, with miniature bed posts at each corner.

What would he look like bound to the posts?

Perhaps that was a game they could play another day, if they decided to explore each other's bodies again. No, thinking about the future, the chances of their liaison being more than a one-night stand, was not something she needed to deal with right now. Could he feel the tremble that threatened to claim her, the fear that she was doing the wrong thing? She didn't know how to dominate someone, no matter how many naughty novels she'd read. It wasn't the same as doing it in real life, and what if she hurt him?

"Sue?" Alan frowned. "Are you all right? You weren't here for a moment. You look a little unsettled."

"I'm fine, really." He didn't deserve her attention being split, especially when he'd done nothing to suggest he would be like the rest of them. She sat down on the edge of the bed, pulling him down to join her.

"Trust me."

"I do." She nodded, a soft shiver running through her body.

"Will you let me love you? Show you what it can be like in the hands of one that thinks you're a beautiful, sensual and strong woman? I've shown you that I trust you, let you take control, now I'm asking you to let me show you how I can touch you." He reached up and cupped her cheek, brushing his thumb along the line of her jaw. "If something doesn't feel right, if you're afraid, or simply want to stop, all you have to do is tell me and it will end."

She leaned into his hand, closing her eyes. "Show me what it's like then. Please."

"Willingly," Alan whispered and pushed her back against the bed.

Why had she given up the control he had so freely offered her earlier in the night?

Because she wasn't a dominatrix, it was one thing to fantasize about a man on his knees, obeying her every whim, but exploring it as more than a passing idea was another matter entirely.

But she wanted to be, a part of her needed to know what it would be like to explore that side of her nature completely. Just one brief step into that world had left her trembling with a need to know more.

His lips brushed over the curves of her breasts. Soft kisses, the wings of a butterfly caressing her flesh as he settled down onto the bed next to her. Her breasts tightened, nipples crinkling into firm points as she let herself sink into the wave of sensation. Men of his age were swift, hungry, eager to satisfy their own needs, yet Alan took his time, exploring her body with a gentle touch. His fingers teased about her nipples, then traced a soft path across her stomach towards her mound.

"Such a beautiful woman. So soft, silken. A real figure. No bones, no harsh edges, just a woman in all her glory." His voice was little more than a hungry whisper against the side of her breast.

"Alan, I'm not beautiful."

"They say that beauty is in the eye of the beholder, and you're very much a glorious, beautiful woman to me."

*Glorious?*

No one had ever called her that before.

"I ..."

"No more words, just relax and try to enjoy it. Please." He teased his fingers through the soft curls that decorated her mound, not quite touching the hidden vee or the small bud hidden within.

Heat claimed her labia, the need to spread her legs, to tempt him to delve between her thighs was almost too much to bear as he closed his lips about one nipple, suckling it deep into his mouth. She groaned; her fingers tightened on the covers beneath her body.

"Please." She murmured, lifting her hips upwards from the bed. Even if he wanted to take things slowly between them, her body already burned with the need to be touched fully, to know his body in intimate detail. "Don't make me wait. Please."

"A little longer."

Why, why did she have to wait at all?

His tongue twirled about the captured nipple. His fingers teased between her lower lips, parting them until he could tap lightly against the hidden nub of sensitive flesh. Each light, swift caress rippled through her core, jerking her hips upwards until she tried to press fully onto his teasing finger.

Her thighs tensed, heels pressed against the bed.

"Do you want more?" His breath, hot and hungry, rolled over her breast.

"Yes!"

"And what do you want, exactly?"

"God, you know. I want you!" Sue whimpered. "I want to feel you inside me."

"You want me to fuck you."

Wicked words, they should have shamed her, but he whispered

them so softly, sensually, with a gentle lick of his tongue against her eager flesh that all she could do was whimper her desire. He didn't stop, the soft tap of that single fingertip against her clit continued as he spoke. She couldn't shut it out, the pressure, the waves of hunger, need, delight, they all rolled into one only to bubble out into a solitary word.

"Yes."

He shifted along the bed, lifting up onto his hands as he looked down at her. He smiled, no hint of cruelty or coldness touched his gaze. His eyes were soft, almost gentle as he eased between her thighs.

Sue shivered at the touch of his thick, eager cock against her inner thigh. Was this what she had been waiting for?

"You can back out. Any time you want."

"I don't want to." She growled, locking her heels behind his ass as she reached out for him. "Make love to me, please."

He thrust into her tight confines with a cry of sheer delight. One she echoed as her inner walls clenched on his erection, lifting her hips to meet that single, filling movement. She groaned, reaching up until she tangled her fingers into his hair and dragged him down to meet her in a deep kiss.

He rolled his hips, stroking her core, teasing her inner walls into life as she clung against him, searching his mouth with her tongue. Each breath she exhaled, he shared. He groaned against her lips and pulled away from the kiss as he gulped for air.

His chest hairs tickled against her breasts.

Her fingers tightened in his hair, but this time she didn't pull him back down for a fresh kiss. Thought no longer answered her call, she reacted to him, rocked with him, matched each thrust will a deep hip roll as her body tightened again and again on his thick, pulsing cock.

Pressure. She couldn't deny it any longer. A heat that came in wave after delicious, near-painful wave, through her body, only to add to the weight. Her inner walls felt it too and tried to clench on his cock until she could have sworn she was trying to push him out. Yet all she wanted was to keep him within her body, until the very end of time if she could just find a way to manage it.

Her vulva rippled once more on his thick erection. Pain, pleasure, pressure, and fear all rolled into one all-consuming crescendo of sensation.

"Need to come," she gasped, her thighs locking about his hips.

"Come for me Sue, please come." He leaned down, brushing his lips against hers. "Come with me! I'm begging you."

That's all she needed to hear. Her back arched from the bed, her heels pressed against the bedding, she rolled with him, bucked as her breath came in short, sharp gulps for air. She couldn't see, passion blinded her vision, claiming it until all she could do was give into it.

Slick heat covered her inner thighs.

His lips parted an inch above hers yet he didn't move.

She screamed, the pressure too much to bear yet she had no choice, even as it rippled free about his cock, binding them, shattering them, destroying and recreating them in one ear-piercing scream they both gave life to.

# *Chapter Eleven*

Alan smiled and held the sleeping woman close. They'd all but collapsed after their shared release and now she snuggled against him and slept peacefully.

Would it be best if he let her sleep through the night?

That part he couldn't be sure about. They both had work the following morning, and she didn't have any clean clothes here. He'd have to either wake her up shortly, or risk disturbing her by reaching out for the alarm clock and setting that for an early jolt first thing in the morning.

He didn't have to make the decision immediately though.

Tomorrow there would be enough to worry about. The blogger ring, the men and women behind the leaks, not to mention the Bill that had caused so much trouble for Sue. It didn't matter that she had apparently been able to deal the man a hell of a blow, he didn't like the idea of anyone picking on her like that.

It just wasn't the type of situation he was willing to let her struggle through alone.

He frowned slightly at the thoughts running through his head. How could he be thinking that way? This was one day, one dinner and a turn in the sack, yet he felt something towards her that was closer to possession?

No, not that, not quite. Something deeper, more important and potentially far more dangerous.

Alan closed his eyes and rested back against the pillows. Comfortable, odd that. He'd never slept with someone through the night, or even for a couple of hours. Strange how at peace he felt holding her like this.

He replayed their night in the back of his mind, every delicious detail. She'd taken control, then stepped back, nervous and uncertain of herself. Had she never taken that role before?

What if he showed her how?

Hope flickered into being.

If she wanted this, needed it the way he did, then he could show her what she would have to learn. It was taking a huge risk, but she was worth it.

* * * * * *

Alan blinked and stared at the ceiling in the darkness. Something leaned against him. No, not something. Someone. A warm, soft someone who cuddled against him.

Sue.

Good, she was still here.

*Shit, I fell asleep. God. What time is it?*

He tried to wriggle away from Sue enough so he could take a look at the clock. Two. Damnit, no matter how much he wanted to spend the rest of the night with her, she didn't have any clothes here.

"Sue." He whispered against the side of her neck. "Sue, wake up love."

She mumbled and cuddled in a little further. The last thing he wanted to do was wake her up, but he was running out of options.

"Sue, you have to wake up, we've got to get you home."

She shook her head a little and blinked. Long strands of hair caught in her eyelashes for a moment before she brushed them aside. "What?"

"Sue, I'm sorry, but it's gone two."

"Shit." She sat up quickly, reaching for the sheets to pull them about her breasts.

"Please, don't hide from me." He caught the edge of the sheet but didn't pull it down. Even in the darkness he could see her, the outline of her face and the deep shadows across her skin caressing her every move.

"I'm just embarrassed. I had no plans for this to happen between us. For the night to end up this way."

His heart sank to the pit of his stomach.

"Oh, you're regretting what happened tonight. I'm sorry ..."

Wonderful, he finally found a woman he could enjoy the time with and she wasn't happy with him.

"No, it's not that. I just don't want you thinking that I'm the sort of woman that jumps into bed with any man that comes along. I'm just not like that." She rolled out of bed, taking the sheet with her. "I'm not a slut."

"I never implied you were, Sue."

"What else could you be thinking about me after the way I acted? I can't even say it was the drink, I only had the one glass of wine -- no, two, there was that second one with the meal." She looked around the room. "Shit, my clothes are -- oh God, my stockings are ruined."

"I'll buy you some new ones." He slipped out of bed and reached for his robe. This was not how he had planned on the night ending. He had to do something to smooth things over for her. Damnit, the last thing he thought her to be was a slut. She was a good woman, strong, beautiful, courageous, and everything he had ever wanted in a woman.

"No, you don't need to do that."

"But I want to, Sue. Just as I want to see you again. I'll get your clothes for you." He fastened the robe about his waist and turned back to look at her. "Sue, are you crying?"

"Please, I just want to go home." She stood there, in the middle of his bedroom, shaking violently. The sheet wrapped about her body, her fingers clutching it tightly. "I think I should get home, Barb will be worried about me and -- and I don't want to be a bother to you. I can call a cab."

Hell, what had they done to her? The men she had been with, the ones in her life prior to tonight, had they treated her like a piece of dirt? A body to fuck then walk out on?

"I'm not like them, I told you that last night. I won't just walk out on you, Sue." He walked back into the main room and picked up her clothing. "I'll take you home, but I want to see you again. After work. Somewhere for coffee, or where you feel safe. But I do want to see you again, more than tonight, more than just one brush-off or after-date meet up. I want to see you as often as you feel comfortable. And if we don't have sex again for weeks, even months, I'll accept that. Shit, if you never feel comfortable having sex with me again I'll understand and agree. I won't like it but I'll not push you."

*Right, I won't push -- much. I'm human for pity's sake.*

She looked so vulnerable standing there. "I want to believe you."

"Then at least give me a chance. I didn't hurt you tonight did I?" He handed off the clothes back to Sue and turned his back to give her a little privacy. "In fact, I'm pretty sure that I went out of my way to give you control."

"I know. I guess I'm just a little worried."

He smiled at the sound of the sheet being dropped to the floor. "Well, I'm guessing that more than a few dates have turned a little sour."

"Too many to count."

"Yet, you trusted me last night."

"Maybe that was a mistake."

"Maybe it wasn't." He didn't turn around, not even when he heard her zipping the dress back up. "There's only one way to find out. Besides, we do need to see each other again, even if it's only to find the ones behind that blogger ring. I don't think you want to let them get away with it."

For a moment she didn't reply. But when she did there was a calm acceptance in her voice that hadn't been there before. "You're right. I don't want them to get away with it."

"Then what do you want me to do?" He tried to keep the desperation from his voice. He had to keep his word, if she wanted to leave, to have nothing more to do with him sexually, he had to accept that.

## Curvaeous Heart

"Take me home and we'll meet tonight. Not a dinner date though, coffee. The Starbucks just down the road from your office. A nice, safe, public place."

Well, it wasn't a complete brush-off. It would give him a chance to work a few things out in his mind, and maybe discover a way to help regain her trust. "Sounds good to me. So will you let me drive you home?"

# *Chapter Twelve*

"What time did you get in last night?" Barb stared up at her from the kitchen table. "I know it was gone one as that's about the time I crawled into bed. I presumed everything was all right or you'd have called, but I have to admit I was a bit worried about you."

"I'm sorry, it was pretty late. Things didn't go exactly the way I planned." Sue admitted and settled down in the spare chair. "I'm not sure what got into me though."

"Well from the looks of your hair, I'd say a good man."

Heat flushed across her face instantly. "Barb!"

"Well, I'm right aren't I?" Her friend grinned. "Come on, tell me what happened. Is he good? I mean scream-all-night-and-into-the-morning good?"

"I can't believe you expect me to go into details." Sue rubbed the sleep from her eyes, or rather a mix of that and gummy stuff that always appeared when she didn't get enough sleep.

"No, I don't. But you can't blame me for teasing you. You obviously enjoyed his company and that says a lot. But something doesn't add up; you look as though you've been crying half the night."

"For an hour at least." Sleep had come reluctantly once Alan had walked her to the door and made sure she was safe. It hadn't mattered just how tired she was, or how good her body felt, not even the kiss -- a brief, soft, sensual kiss good night -- had managed to ease her mood. Instead she'd lain on the bed, staring at the ceiling, going over all the mistakes she'd made that night.

Had she made any mistakes? Or was it just her imagination?

He'd enjoyed it, she had, he wanted to see her again. So just why had she spent the rest of the night staring at the paintwork?

"Spill, what's the problem -- oh shit, he didn't dump you did he? I'll kill him!"

## Curvaeous Heart

"No, it's not that. I just  --  I don't think I can risk seeing him again on my own. I made such a terrible mistake and I don't want to repeat it. He wants to meet up after work tonight; can you go with me?"

*Meet him and maybe eat him?*

Sue almost choked at the deliciously evil thoughts her mind was all too ready to supply.

"Slow down. What sort of mistake?" Barb pushed up from the small table long enough to fill a fresh mug of coffee and place it in front of Sue. "Is he a jerk? Did he take what he wanted and then leave you waiting? Don't tell me he's one of those men who rolls over and starts to snore without thinking about you? Fuck. I wouldn't have put him down as that type."

"No, he's a good man, at least from what I've seen. If I'd have told him to stop at any point he'd have ended it and not made me feel horrible for changing my mind." How many men were like that? Not many, from what she'd seen so far. Most grabbed what they could and ran for the door.

"Okay, is he on the make, after money?"

"No, he's wealthy, the whole son-of-the-boss thing isn't just a work place advantage. He's got a nice home, decent clothes, good taste in food." The bed, the couch, the crackling fireplace, she could have stayed there forever.

"Does he have bad breath?"

"No, of course not!"

"Then just what's the problem?"

"I am. Shit. I jumped right into bed with him."

Barb frowned, opened her mouth to speak, closed it again, shook her head, and then laughed. "Is that all you're worried about?"

"Well he's going to think that I'm easy."

"Sue, I'd have jumped into bed with him. I'd still think about it given half the chance, but he's not interested in me. Even if I was the type to go behind a friend's back, he'd turn me down." Barb set her mug down on the table and rubbed her temples. "I know you're afraid, but after last night you shouldn't be. There's nothing wrong in finding someone attractive and going for it with them. You enjoyed it, he did from the look on your face, so what's wrong with being human and admitting that it was fun?"

Sue shifted in her seat and dropped her gaze to the coffee. "I don't know. I just -- well I guess I thought he'd be disgusted when he realized what we did and when he asked to see me again I was shocked."

Shocked, that was putting it mildly.

"When are you going to accept that you're beautiful? Couldn't you see it in his eyes last night?"

Sue sucked in her bottom lip and chewed on it. He had looked at her as if she were something special. Those small touches to her fingers through dinner, the heated looks, the way he had escorted her out through the restaurant as if he were the luckiest man on the planet. Yet a part of her still didn't want to believe it had all happened.

"So you think I'm being stupid?"

"I think you're letting your fears get the better of you."

Fears. Such small things yet they wanted to rule her life. "What if he's like David? I don't think I could take that again."

"How will you know if he's a better man if you don't take the risk? You made the first step, and second, last night."

Second, third, and maybe fourth. They hadn't exactly kept things meek and mild last night. She took a small sip of the drink, cupping the mug back and forth between her hands.

Had he really called her ma'am?

"What are you thinking about?"

"Just, well maybe I didn't make a mistake after all."

"Only one real way to find out, isn't there?"

"Yes, I know." There was no escaping that. It didn't make sense. She'd never been the type to just jump into bed with someone. And never on a first date, yet with him, with Alan, it felt right. "I could give him a call. See if he wants to make that a lunch meeting."

"Or you could wait until after work and get a few things done. Make sure this isn't something you're doing just to try and fit in with the world. I'm not saying that you did anything wrong. Quite the opposite in fact, but if you rush things, change dates around, then you'll start questioning yourself."

"Huh? Sorry I'm not quite sure I understand." Maybe she just hadn't had enough sleep. Or not enough caffeine.

"If you change when you're meeting him, rush off to spend time with him, you'll then wonder if you're doing it because you want to, or because it feels like the thing you're supposed to do. I don't know if that makes sense to you." Barb rested her head on her hands and let her hair fall over her face. "Gawd. I need some more coffee in my system before I start handing out advice first thing in the morning."

"You need to get some food in you, coffee, and hit the shower. Shit, so do I. We're going to be late at this rate, and the last thing either of us need is a black mark on our files." Taking yesterday morning off had been difficult enough. Still, they'd pulled it off and the risk had been worth it.

Alan had been worth it.

"You're getting that dreamy look on your face again." Barb reached for the sugar and added a little more to the cup. "Go take your shower, I need some more caffeine before I even think about stepping into one."

Sue tried not to laugh, but stood up and rolled out her shoulders. Every inch of her skin felt alive, tingling in places she had long since forgotten. "Fine, I'll take the shower first and you try and get out of the zombie state, or at least to the point where you can stand up under the shower without falling asleep."

"Bitch." Barb laughed.

"Yes, I think I am and I love being one." Still laughing, more to herself than anything else, Sue hurried out of the kitchen.

*Please, Ma'am.*

Yes, he'd said it, teased her with the thought of being a dominant, and by God she'd enjoyed it. What would it be like if she took it a step further? And where would she go to learn what to do? There had to be books out there, places she could research. She had a computer so there was always the Net, but what if he didn't want her like that?

A long, hot shower. Just what she needed before she went to work, though a part of her didn't want to wash his scent from her body.

Hot water pelted against her skin minutes later; the large shower stall had been one of the reasons they had agreed to rent the place. Too many homes these days came with tiny bathrooms, or miniscule showers, and even if she hadn't been a larger woman the idea of taking a shower in a coffin-sized area would have been less than appealing.

Sue leaned back against the tile-covered wall, closing her eyes as she turned the shower head on her face. Who needed a facial with a good massage setting like that?

What was Alan doing now?

Would he be on the way to work, or already in his office? Did he go for a run first thing in the morning? He looked like the type of man that worked out when he had the chance. He'd certainly felt that way.

She smiled, shaking her head softly before she ducked her head under the water, wetting it down before working the shampoo into her hair.

Heat rippled through her inner walls as the needlelike caress of the water teased her body.

Turned on by the shower?

No, that wasn't possible, was it?

Her nipples ached, tightening into taut, small buds that begged to be touched.

Not fair, she didn't have time to do anything about it. Not with work, with Barb needing the shower once she'd finished off. Shit, what was she supposed to do now?

Live with it?

She squirmed, her thighs pressed tightly together as she reached for the soap and tried to focus on cleaning off. She could almost feel his touch again, across her breasts, over her stomach, small light nips around her nipples.

Sue groaned, building up the lather on her hand before she shifted a little to wash between her thighs only to pull back her hand in shock. Hot. She'd never felt so warm there before. It would have been so very easy to slide her finger between her lower lips and tease her ...

Fuck, she was running out of time, and no matter how horny she now felt she wasn't about to get them both into trouble.

* * * * * *

She was late.

Alan checked his watch for the third time in the last ten minutes.

What was keeping her? She'd agreed to meet him and she'd called him at the office only a few hours earlier to confirm she'd meet him for coffee just as they'd planned, so where was she?

Maybe she'd changed her mind at the last minute? She had sounded tired when they'd spoken. Had her night, once he had escorted her home, been as disturbed as his had been?

Every time he had tried to sleep he'd been disturbed by dreams of her changing on him. Going from the woman he had seen enjoying her first taste of dominating another human being, into one who laughed and mocked him for his desires.

No, she wasn't like that.

Alan closed his eyes and tried to relax. Years of his father trying to push him into dates with women he wanted nothing to do with. For the most part he'd been able to avoid them, or tell his dad no, and repeat the no until he actually took notice. Or did so for a short time at least.

Now he had a chance with a woman he felt something real towards.

Love? Perhaps, but it was too soon to say that. Far too soon, if he mentioned it to Sue then she'd back away slowly and look for the hidden cameras. It didn't matter how real the feelings were towards her, it just wasn't the right time to tell her.

So when would be?

After they made love again? If she let him near her any time soon?

His cock thickened at the thought of her naked body lying next to him in the bed. Her eyes closed, those thick lashes caressing the curves of her cheeks. So innocent. And yet hungry. Oh God, she'd been hungry for his touches.

His thighs ached and he shifted in the chair. It would have been so very easy to just reach into his pants and wrap his hand around his cock. If he hadn't been in the middle of a very public place, that is.

"Alan?"

He sat up quickly, opening his eyes only to see Sue standing on the other side of the table. Just as well that he had the table between them, this way she wouldn't see the growing tent in his pants.

"Did you fall asleep?"

"No, sorry I was just going over a few things from work." He wasn't exactly lying, he had met her at work and they'd certainly put a great deal of effort into pleasing each other. "I wasn't sure you were going to make it after all."

"I'd have called you, left a message at the office if plans had changed." Sue gave a quick look at the empty chair. "Did you want me to sit down?"

"This works just fine. After all I want you to be comfortable." Naked, sprawled out on his bed with his cock buried between her thighs, that's what he really wanted. "And I don't think you're ready for being in a more private place with me again, not yet at least."

It didn't stop him from wanting that, needing it. Her body, his, the two blended together.

She eased down into the chair, a slight smile settling into place. "You're the most amazing man I've ever met."

"Now that's something I haven't heard in a long time." Amazing? Why, because he'd treated her as a human being. A wonderful, deliciously sensual human being?

"Not sure why, but then again since meeting you I've learned that there are a lot of men out there who don't treat women with the greatest of respect. So, why did you want to see me again today? Like this I mean?"

"I wanted you to know you were safe with me. That I didn't just want to see you only for  --  well for sex." That sounded awkward, even to him. Wonderful, she'd think he'd turned into wonder dork. Where had his ability to form a coherent sentence vanished to?

A soft laugh drew his attention back to Sue's eyes. "I'm sorry, that just sounded so weird coming from you. Of course I know I'm safe, if I wasn't you wouldn't have wanted to meet me again at all. And what's wrong with meeting someone for just sex every now and then?"

His heart skipped a beat as his cock throbbed into life. "Now that's something I wasn't expecting to hear from you either. Not that I'm complaining."

"I didn't think you would." She rested her elbows on the table, cupping her chin in her hand. Long strands of hair half fell over her face, veiling it for a moment until she swept it back from her eyes. "Not that I'm suggesting we should head for somewhere more private."

Not yet at least, but there was something in the way she smiled at him. A glimpse of a mischief, hunger, or something else that he didn't quite recognize. Whatever it was it looked good on her. A light flickered in her eyes, she smiled, but it wasn't the soft, playful smile or friendly welcome he was used to seeing on a woman. One corner of her mouth twitched upwards, a dimple half forming in her cheek as she peered at him through her lashes.

Coy.

What he wouldn't have given for the chance to show her just what that look did to him.

"And what if I asked you to come home with me again, Sue?"

"I thought you wanted to give me some time?" Her voice was soft, tempting as she leaned forward a little more on the table. "I have a lot to think about, after what happened, what we did -- there are some things I'm not certain about."

"I know, sorry. Just that I..." His palms felt sweaty. What was happening to him? He wasn't like this around women normally.

"Just what?"

*Just I want to pull you over the table, say screw the world, and lick every luscious part of your body until you scream my name.*

"I find you attractive, sorry about that." He blushed, for the first time since leaving high school, he actually blushed.

Her gaze narrowed, the tiny lines around her eyes crinkling. Another woman might have hidden them, taken the time and wasted the money with plastic surgery, but not Sue. She was real, she accepted who she was, every small fault, every touch of age, her soft, comforting body that opened up so readily for him.

Some would have called her obese; they were wrong. She was healthy, strong, and at peace with herself. Even if she wanted to spend some time in a gym it wouldn't change the core of who she was, just tighten her up in places.

His cock surged against the pressure of his pants, the thickening erection far more than he had been expecting to cope with.

"Nothing to be sorry about, actually it's kind of nice." Sue reached out across the table, heat coloring her cheeks. The confidence slipped away, just as it had the night before, and for a moment he saw it again. That soft vulnerability that called to him. Would it have been so wrong to move around the table and wrap his arms about her?

*How could she be vulnerable and strong all at the same time? He wanted to protect her, and yet kneel at her feet. Damn, talk about being mixed up.*

"So what now? Do we have that coffee and get to know each other a little better, or do you head for home and leave me to it?"

Sue's brow crinkled into a slight frown. "I thought you wanted more information about the blogger ring?"

"I do, but I also know you're not willing to risk your friends, which I can understand." Sooner or later it would come out though. There'd be no other choice, Sue had to know that. "I think I can track him down myself. I've got our internet security people looking into it, but without a court order the owners of the blogger site don't have to do anything to help us. At most they'll shut down the sites if we report them for violating the terms of services."

Her eyes began to glaze around the time he got to the TOS side of things.

"I'm boring you."

"No, you're not, it's just that you're talking about things that sound a lot like work to me." Sue winked, the dazed look vanishing from her gaze as quickly as it had appeared.

"Oh, you're bad."

"I think you've got a fairly good idea of just how bad I can be when the need arises."

That he couldn't argue with. "Ah, but was that just a one-off?"

"Why don't we find somewhere a little more private to find out? And -- well there are some other things I want to talk to you about as well. About last night. Some of the things we did, I mean I did." Sue faltered for a moment then looked him straight in the eyes. "I tried something with you last night, something I've never done before, though I've dreamed of it, and I need to know if -- if that's something you want more of?"

# *Chapter Thirteen*

"Are you sure you want to do this?" Alan spoke quietly, giving her fingers a quick squeeze. "You don't have to. And we did say we'd take this time to let you think things through, or ..."

"We did it this way so I wouldn't keep thinking you'd dump me after getting me into bed. Well, I'm nearly forty, I'm not a child, and if I don't stop jumping at shadows, expecting every man to dump me, then I'll never be able to enjoy my life. And quite frankly, I don't want to live that way."

Forty wasn't the end of the world, but she wasn't a child any longer either. It was about damn time she did something with her life instead of sitting on her ass waiting for the world to change around her. It wasn't going to do that unless she forced it to change. And the very first person she had to work on was the one that looked back at her from the mirror every morning.

So what if she would never be a size 5 or 7 or, hell, a 12, it didn't matter unless she wanted to worry about it.

"Then I'd be an idiot to turn you down." He glanced down at his lap, then back at her. "I've been trying to keep my body under control since you sat down and I've failed miserably. All I've been able to think about was just how good you felt, how you moaned when I touched you, the feel of your lips around my cock and -- well, I'm damn glad you've decided to say screw the world."

"No, not screw the world. The person I want to do that to is you, or rather, erm, you know what I mean." Her cheeks flushed crimson, liquid heat coated her inner walls, and she could feel her panties growing damp. "Look, I still need to know if what we did, beyond the final result, is something you like?"

"Yes, I do." Alan pushed back from the table and grinned. "I mean I did. You've no idea how many times I've dreamed of a woman who was willing and able to -- well, take charge. Shit, that sounds lame, I know. It's a world I've explored only through chats, talking to people, I've never met someone I've felt comfortable enough with to take it further. Most women just laugh at the idea of a man like me wanting to…"

"Wait, take a breath, and think. We need to take this conversation somewhere more private." Was he insane? What if someone heard them, heard him? How would he deal with the funny looks he would get? Or the mocking comments?

"Agreed." He murmured.

Her gaze lowered slowly to his groin. The outline of his cock pressed all too clearly against his pants even as he grabbed the newspaper from the table and used it to half shield his arousal. "Not that I mind you knowing, but unless you want to advertise what we're about to do to the world…?"

A part of her wanted to take out an ad on every television channel she could find and scream out that she was about to get fucked until she passed out, but he had a point. She wasn't the type that let others know what was going on, even if it seemed like a good idea at the time.

"Well, it might get us kicked out of the store, never to return, and I'd miss the coffee." She winked and took his free hand, entwining her fingers with his. "So where are we going? Your place or mine?"

"Mine, it's closer. Unless you have any objections?"

His home, with its wonderful bed, or hers, with her laundry in a pile in the corner of the room. Decisions, decisions.

"Yours works just fine with me."

His grip tightened on her hand as they walked out of the coffee shop, not enough to hurt but a possessive clutch that sent a deep clench through her inner walls. Was it just his state of arousal or did he want her in other ways?

*I don't know and I don't care right now.*

Not entirely true. Something else was slowly growing in the pit of her stomach. A desire she didn't want to admit to. One that had caused her to stumble more than once. The need to hear a word from his lips, four letters, short, sweet and oh so very dangerous.

*Does it really matter if this is love or lust just as long as it's something I want and enjoy?*

A month ago love would have been a factor from the very start, but...

"Sue, you've no idea how lucky I feel right now." Alan murmured as he unlocked the car for her. "I'm not going to start making promises to you, or declarations, but I want you to know that it means a lot to me that you trust me."

Trust, lust, the two did blur into each other at times. Though she'd smacked more than a few friends over the back of the head for mistaking the boundary between the two.

*Hey, I'm not mistaking it, I'm just ignoring it!*

"Well if it turns out you're one of those fuck-them-and-leave-them types, I do know where you live and I can come and hunt you down." Sue winked and slipped into the passenger seat.

"If I hurt you then I'll hand you a belt and you can take it to my ass."

Now there was a delicious image indeed. "Don't tempt me."

"Ah, yes. Your kinky side."

"I don't have a kinky side." She protested, the words half dying as she twisted in her seat to look him fully in the eyes. "Not much of one anyway."

"You do. You just want to ignore it. If you didn't you wouldn't have got such a kick out of me standing still and doing what you wanted last night. And even you admitted it was something you wanted to discuss with me."

"Hey, are you trying to tell me that I'm some sort of dominant?" Now that didn't make sense, not from the way she'd let men walk over her on more than one occasion. Except she'd enjoyed it, the control, the time with him and there was no denying the stories she preferred to read.

"No, I'm saying you like to play the game on occasions. I guess you'd be -- just new to all of this, or perhaps a switch? I've done a little looking into this over the years, I won't hide the fact that I've enjoyed the idea of finding a strong woman who could explore that with me." He slipped the key into the ignition and started the car up. "Standing there, learning to control myself, letting you set the pace like that, was erotic. In more ways than I care to admit to right now."

He purred the last word and her hips twitched. What would it be like to feel his lips around her clit? That soft purr vibrating into her tight bud? Her vulva trembled and tried to close on the cock it wanted buried between her walls, but couldn't have. Not just yet at least.

"Erotic. And powerful. I'd never been given the chance to do that before."

"Well it worked very well for both of us. Perhaps I should let you set the pace again?" He glanced over, weaving the car through the traffic. "And I'm betting you've thought about doing something like that. You took charge easily, at least once you'd set your mind to it."

"Yes, well maybe a little." Sue admitted, trembling slightly. Was she truly that easy to read? "I've got a small collection of novels stacked in my room that cover situations like this."

"Now that doesn't surprise me at all."

"So you truly didn't mind my taking over?"

"Not at all. If it had been in any way uncomfortable I'd have said something but -- well you saw the results."

Yes, she had.

"So don't let that worry you. We both enjoyed it and perhaps once we're a little more settled it's something we can explore to-gether. I know you're uncertain, I am as well, but we can do this together."

Sue shifted a little on the seat, glancing out of the window. Ex-plore being a dominant? Or was he talking about just playing the game, a few turns in the bedroom?

"You're unsettled by all of this?"

"A little."

"I can understand that," he reached over and squeezed her knee. "So just what is going through your mind right now?"

"You don't want to know."

"Yes, I do."

"It's embarrassing."

"Not to me."

"Hm, and if I said I wanted you to lick me until I came?" Why hadn't she tried being this way before? She was an adult, and it wasn't as though she hit on men for sex before now. Shit, most of the time she waited until they had been going out for a while before she let them get this far.

Was that the reason they left her?

*Hey, idiot, stop thinking that way. They left because they're ignorant wankers who got what they wanted and left you to it. They weren't good enough. They were the problem, not you!*

Alan turned down a small road, past a fish and chip shop as the car filled, for a brief moment, with the tempting smell of malt vinegar and fresh chips. For the first time in months it didn't call to her the way it normally did.

"You give me the image of spending time between your thighs, licking you, tasting you, and you want to know what I think about it? It sounds like just the sort of meal I'd go back for second helpings on."

God, he was just as wicked as she was.

As she had always been but had been too afraid to let out until now.

"Then we could always make this a three course meal."

* * * * * *

Alan unlocked his front door and took a step back, letting Sue in ahead of him, inhaling deeply as she walked past. Musk, female musk, he could smell it, almost taste it on the air. She'd squirmed in the seat next to him for the majority of the short trip and now he knew why.

Just how turned on was she?

He followed her in and locked the door behind him. "Now what am I going to do with you again? Give you a foot rub? Discuss money, or terms of services again? I could put you to sleep with all the interesting details in just how shipping is handled for overseas and the custom forms."

Sue groaned and shot him a hard look. "You do that and I'll take you up on using the belt against your ass."

"And if I wasted our time on that then I'd deserve every single stroke." He chuckled and slid up behind her, wrapping his arms about her waist as he nuzzled against her neck. "You taste so sweet here, I wonder what you'll taste like a little lower down?"

"Why don't we find out?" She glanced back up at him over her shoulder. "That's if you still want to. I don't want to push you into something you're not ready for. After all, you might really want to go over something from work, or the blogger ring, and not risk being hurt by me."

Had she really pushed aside her doubts?

He tried looking into her eyes, to see if there was anything there that should have been a warning to him to back off, take his time, give her a little more space despite what she'd told him.

His cock twitched at the blatant hunger in her gaze.

*Oh yeah, she wants this, as much as I do, if not more. And she's not kidding about the dominance either.*

Women wanting him was something he had become used to, but it had never been like this. She wasn't looking at him as marriage bait, neither had she been set up by his father. This was different, they both wanted it, needed it, and...

No, he wasn't going to say the word. Not yet at least. Feel it, slowly accept it deep inside, but not say it. How many others had used that word, a lie, a mockery of what he felt in order to get what they wanted from her?

"Did you want anything to drink?" He took a step away from her but didn't get any further than that as she grabbed hold of his arm. "I'd be happy to serve you."

"Later. What I want is you." She trembled slightly, little more than a tiny shiver or shake that he almost missed. "Please."

Alan closed the gap between them and wrapped his arms tightly about her, whispering into her hair. "Whatever you want."

"You've no idea just how much I want."

"Maybe you'll tell me one day?"

She looked up, brushing his lips with hers in a soft, tender kiss. Her breasts pressed against his chest as she slid her arms about his neck, nipples hard even through her clothing. She whimpered, shifting against his cock, which surged back into life, throbbing against her body.

"You're wearing too many clothes." She murmured against his lips, nibbling at them.

He shuddered, trying to keep control of his body, but his cock had other ideas. Each touch, breath, shift of weight between them only added to the heaviness in his tightening sac. His erection threatened to burst through his pants if he didn't do something about it soon, and he'd promised to bring her to climax first.

Not that he regretted his choice, but at this rate he'd be ready to come the minute he entered her. If not before.

"Maybe we should do something about that then?" He reached for the buttons on her blouse, a simple piece of cream lightweight cotton, and undid them as she nipped at his throat. "Are you going to help out?"

"I thought I'd let you undress me, seeing as I did a striptease for you last time."

He groaned, the image of her standing in front of him in nothing more than her stockings and suspender belt had almost been too much to bear. Did they even sell those belts anymore? Obviously, if she'd been able to track one down. Ah, of course, the miracle of the Net with the aid of a credit card.

### *Curvaeous Heart*

The blouse parted under his fingers until it lay open, baring her bra-covered breasts to his view. It would have been so very easy to cup them, strip them bare, but he resisted the urge and rested his hands on her shoulders.

"Then you're right, it is my turn. If you can stand still for it?"

"You think I can't?" One almost delicate eyebrow arched upwards.

"I'm not sure, I think it will be a struggle for you." He traced one finger down the length of her spine, until he cupped her ass. She shivered against him, eyes half closing, lips parted in a soft O.

"You managed it last night."

"Maybe I have more will power than you."

"Or maybe I've learned to have more control over my body than you have of yours." She swallowed hard, a soft tremor in her voice. "I'm older, wiser, and I know where my limits are."

"You know where some of them are." His other hand slid slowly down her back in low, curling circles over the back of her blouse. "There are always other limits, strengths and weaknesses waiting to be discovered."

Sue leaned against him, closing her eyes. Her body tense beneath his fingers; soft, delicious trembles working their way through her back; her breath catching in the back of her throat. "And what do I get if I manage to keep still whilst you undress me?"

"My heart?" He whispered into her hair, only half teasing. It would have been so very easy to tell her how he felt, but it wasn't the right time. "Except I don't think you're a man-eater like that. So what do you want?"

"A promise."

An invisible hand wrapped around his heart. "Oh?"

"A promise, that when I call in the debt you will answer one question honestly, without reservation. No matter what it is."

A dangerous promise. She could try and find out about a deal at work, turn into another power-hungry woman who only wanted to control everything he had, or did. Except, she wasn't like that. She didn't give off that vibe. The only thing she appeared to be hungry for was him.

"All right then. I promise."

"Then do your worst." Sue lifted her head and stepped back barely more than two inches. "I won't move unless you tell me to until you've finished stripping me down."

He grinned, looking her over as he released his hold on her. Would she really be able to stay still? There was only one way to find out.

"Then close your eyes."

"Hmmm? Going to see just how much I can take?"

"Well, if we're going to make this a challenge there's no point taking it easy on you, is there?" Her blouse lay open and now that he'd moved back from her just a little he could see the soft mounds of her breasts peeking out above the white cups of her bra. It was a myth that a large woman or older woman ended up with breasts hanging down to their waist. No, hers were not the firm, perky things of a twenty-year-old, but they still had their shape, some level of firmness to them, and she didn't appear to be bothered by the weight of them.

One thing he'd noticed earlier on was that Sue didn't slouch. She stood tall, proud, with her shoulders back. So many larger women slumped their shoulders, or tried to make themselves look smaller when they stood up. Maybe that was one of the reasons she looked firmer. She carried herself well.

"So are you going to stand there all day, or actually do something?"

"Impatient, are you?" He tried not to laugh and reached out, tracing tiny circular patterns over the upper curves of her breasts. Even now there was a commanding tone behind her words. One that he struggled not to instantly obey. He'd never liked this about a woman before, but he wanted to drop to his knees and kiss her feet. They had to talk, once their desires had been satisfied, for a short time at least. They truly had to talk about their shared interests. "Maybe I like to take my time in unwrapping a present?"

"Oh, I'm a gift now am I?'

"Oh yes, one I plan on savoring every single step of the way." He twitched at the edges of her blouse, letting the fabric lift upwards, away from her body, before it rested back against her skin. The soft contact was enough to bring a fresh shiver, tiny goose bumps raising under the path of his fingers.

Was it cold?

No, it didn't feel cold. Good, then his touches were having the right effect.

Her nipples poked against the cups of the bra, tempting him. It would have been so very easy to reach out and brush against them. His fingers itched and he had to yank his hands back away from her body before he gave into temptation.

He slipped out of his shoes and walked quietly around her until he looked at her back. She tensed at the slight sound, frowning, straining to hear what was going on. Good, she wasn't entirely sure where he was.

"Nervous?" He leaned in and whispered against the back of her neck.

Sue half jumped, and clenched her fists. "Rotten bastard."

"And you love it." Alan caught the back of her blouse and eased it down over her shoulders, then down her arms until he dropped it on the floor. "You're enjoying this, learning more about yourself and what you like, yet you don't know what's coming next, where I'm going to touch you or what I'm going to do beyond stripping you."

She sucked in her bottom lip, chewing on it.

"And you're nervous."

"So were you."

He couldn't argue that point. He reached down and unhooked her skirt. "No stockings today though?"

"Tights instead."

He bit back a groan as he looked over her, the skirt pooling on the floor. Her legs were covered by the thin, almost silken covering of a pair of nearly black tights. The thin nylon clung to her legs, covering her panties. He shivered, stroking her legs. Smooth, tempting, even the tiny imperfections, the small snarls and black lines where the tights had caught on something, only added to his desire to strip them from her.

She groaned as he stroked her legs, caressing them lightly down from her ass to her ankles until he settled down on his knees in front of her. How could anyone look sexy in tights? Well she managed it.

*It's not what's she's wearing, or doing, it's her. Sue. Everything about her.*

He reached up and hooked his fingers into the top of her tights and eased them down over her hips, carefully exposing the soft skin beneath. Her scent filled his nostrils, the delight of an aroused woman so close to him only served to add to his own growing need. Yet he controlled himself as he lifted her feet up slowly, one at a time, and eased the nylon from her delicate toes.

Heat, he could feel it through her panties, calling to him, begging that he strip them from her and delve into her sex with tongue and fingers alike.

She didn't move, except at his direction, her breathing ragged, thighs trembling as she struggled to hold position. Did it really feel that intense to her? Each touch, each light caress? The dampness he could see in her panties said yes.

He leaned up on his knees, reaching upwards to catch the edge of her bra with his fingers, his teeth nipping at her panties until he knew he had a firm hold on the material. She groaned, her weight shifting slightly from one foot to the other, not enough to break position but the struggle ever more apparent with each passing moment.

He teased his fingers across her firm nipples then pulled at her bra, bringing the cups down, baring her breasts to the delight of his fingers even as he tugged on her panties with his teeth.

"God!" She gasped as he pulled her panties down, dragging his nails over her body, the scratches light, barely enough to raise red lines on her skin, yet she arched into the touch, her heels almost leaving the floor until she forced her body back under control.

"You almost lost it there," he murmured, taking hold of her panties in his hands and slipping them down from her body fully. He rocked back to his feet, chuckling softly as he undid her bra and let it drop to the floor. "But you made it, Sue. You can move again."

"Good." She groaned. "I wasn't sure I could hold in place any longer."

"And when do I get to taste you?" His cock threatened to push through his pants if he didn't do something about the pressure in his body soon.

"When you're ready to." Her gaze trailed down the full length of his body, lingering on the outline of his cock, a wicked smile claiming her lips. "Though from the looks of things perhaps we should move onto something else?"

"But I thought -- Oh!" He cried out as she wrapped her hand around his cock through his pants, squeezed once, and then released her hold on his body. God, how could he ignore her change of heart?

"Strip." She purred.

His hands moved to his pants before he had the chance to think his actions through. His cock ached with the need to feel her body wrapped around it, those tight, slick walls, a ripple of delight and promise of far more if given the chance.

"I want you." He shrugged out of his pants.

"I know."

"I need you." He reached for her arms, pulling her close even as he kicked off his pants and underpants fully and stood there only in his shirt.

"You're insane." A wry smile twitched her lips, a moment of sadness flickered across her eyes and it was gone.

"Maybe I am, but that doesn't change the way I feel." He was getting dangerously close to saying something that could ruin everything between them. Before his mouth got the better of him he cleared what little gap there was between them and wrapped his arms about her. His lips closed on hers as she gasped, arching into his touch.

*Hot, willing, and mine.*

With a low growl, he moved them both back towards the rug in front of the fire. They didn't need the bed, not this time, but he did need her. Now. Not five minutes later, but here and now.

"Alan." She murmured, not fighting his choice. "God, I've never felt this way before." Her thighs parted, letting him settle between them, her fingers teasing at the soft curls on his chest.

"Do you want me to stop?" *Please don't tell me to stop. I'll do it, but please don't.*

"No, not now, not ever." She arched, tipping her hips. "Please, don't make me wait."

He didn't.

With a low, deep moan he eased into her body, shuddering as her walls clenched on his cock. Liquid velvet, heat, silk, he'd heard the terms before, but no two women were the same. There was no real term, no way of describing how it felt to have a woman's sex wrapped about his cock, but his mind still tried to provide the words.

At least it did until she twisted her hips and all but danced on his erection.

Thought fled. A dozen muscled fingers clenched on his body, massaging his cock as he rocked within her. Her nipples scraped his chest, her breath caressed his lips as she wrapped her arms about his neck.

He drew back, until only the tip of his cock was still in her body, gasping. He had to find some level of focus, a way of keeping control, but she had other ideas. Sue pressed her heels behind his ass and tugged him back into her welcoming sex.

He groaned, fighting to keep some level of control as his balls tightened, his sac heavy, full, aching as the need built up in the pit of his stomach. His thighs shook, ass tightening, and still the ball of heated pressure surged upwards into his pulsing cock until he knew what little control he had left was about to be lost.

"Sue!"

"Come for me." She leaned up, nipping at his neck. Her body tightened, released him only to tighten again. The catch in her breath letting him know that he wasn't the only one who was ready to come. "I want to hear you, feel you come for me."

His body responded before his mind had the chance to protest.

Alan cried out, his thighs tight, body taut as he thrust fully into her, shuddering as his body denied all pretense of control in a series of long, trembling jolts of pleasure until he collapsed down against her and rested his head on her breasts.

# *Chapter Fourteen*

"Alan?" She shifted a little beneath him. "We can't stay like this all night. No matter how nice it feels."

He looked up, blinking a little. Had she really worn him out that quickly? They were both tired from the night before. Not enough sleep, all that sex, and she wasn't young anymore but that didn't explain his sleepy and sated expression.

Odd, with other men she'd always been annoyed at the quick sex acts, the grunt-and-cum types, except this was different. He'd taken the time to build her up, arouse her, take care of her and would have done more if she hadn't insisted on pushing things to sex when she had.

But he wasn't like a typical man either.

She ran her fingers gently through his hair. "I need to get up and shower. That way I'm not feeling uncomfortable when we talk."

Alan rested his hands on the floor before easing out of her body and pushing back up to his feet. "Let me help you up, love."

She frowned slightly but quickly smoothed the expression away. Love? Had he just called her love? It wasn't the first time either from what she could remember. No, he didn't mean anything by it, just a habit, or a manner of address by him.

So why did her heart miss a beat when he used it towards her?

*Because a part of me wants the word to mean something coming from him.*

"Did you want to be alone in the shower?"

"Yes, I think so." She nodded and tried to smile. "You know women, we need to wash off, get cleaned up after sex. Most of the time, at least."

"You mean when you haven't just passed out?" He teased and sneaked an arm about her waist. "Come on, let's get you that shower."

## *Curvaeous Heart*

She leaned into his touch, enjoying the sense of peace she felt in his arms. No tension, no concerns, except for that one little word that could bring her so many problems.

A slight smile tugged at the corners of her lips and she opened the shower, turning the water on as she took the towel from Alan. "Thanks, I won't be long."

"Take as long as you need, I'm not going to rush you." He pulled out an oversized toweling robe and set it on the counter. "I'll shower when you're done and then we can have something to eat, maybe sit and talk for a bit."

God, there it was. Something going on between them, time to end it?

*No, he's not going to end it. This is something else. Come on you've been pushing him to talk, so that's all he wants to do. It's time to face that little demon inside. That need he's awoken. There's no going back from it.*

"Is there something the matter?"

"No, quite the opposite in fact. I want to talk to you about the problems with the blogger ring. I think I have an answer but I'll need your help. I also need to talk to you about our shared need."

A shared need. That was one way of putting it. Did he truly need to explore this odd situation between them, or was he just being nice? No, the look in his eyes, the tone of his voice, it was a real enough desire.

How was she supposed to learn though? With him?

It was better than trying to stumble along alone.

And he wanted to be with her.

"Then I won't be long." She ducked into the shower, letting the warm water hit her body.

For a moment he stood there, outside of the stall, watching her. Normally that invasion of privacy might have made her uncomfortable, or would have made her turn so her back was to him. Not this time. Sue smiled at him through the dimpled glass and let him watch until he was ready to leave.

Comfortable. At peace. Accepted.

They were more than just words now.

Did things like this happen so quickly under normal circumstances? She'd heard about love at first sight, who hadn't, but it wasn't actually supposed to happen.

*Admit it, silly. You love him. It's not just lust. You really love him.*

All right, she did. So what?

*So tell him.*

No, she wasn't ready for that yet. Another couple of days, weeks maybe. Just enough time so she could figure out if this really was what she wanted. If this man, this wonderful man young enough to almost be her son, was the one she wanted to spend her life with and then...

Then what?

She frowned and reached for the shampoo, washing off her hair.

*Ask him to marry me? Do women do that now?*

Some did, the brave ones, women who had the confidence to follow through every dream, every hope. She didn't have that strength.

*Yes, I do. All I have to do is stop questioning every damn thing.*

* * * * * *

She poured the steaming water over the hot chocolate mix and stirred it slowly.

"I see you found everything you needed." He rested one hand on her shoulder, squeezing gently. "Would you like to sit down with me for a while? I think we need to talk."

"About the ring, yes you mentioned that."

"More than that." He leaned against the kitchen counter. "And the ring can wait for a moment. I want to talk about you and me, how we both seem to need something here."

Sue pulled out one of the kitchen chairs and settled down at the table, looking up at him. How many heart-to-heart conversations had she shared with Barb at their kitchen table? More than she cared to count.

"You know what D/s means?" Alan picked the chair opposite her. "And some of the other terms involved, like limits, red flags, safe words?"

"I think so, dominance and submission, right?" She took a moment to think about the rest of it. "Limits, they're things a person cannot or will not do, or go past. Red flags I'm not sure of, and safe words are code words used to stop play of any sort?"

Alan nodded. "Right. Red flags are signs, warning signs, in a person that may mark them as being dangerous. Such as saying, as either a dominant or submissive, that you have no limits, or that they aren't needed."

All right, that made sense. "And you think that I'm...?"

"That you're a dominant, or rather a woman with dominant tendencies. I don't know how far that goes, but I've seen it very clearly in how you react around me."

Sue cracked a smile. "I've never explored it with anyone other than you. I've just spent a lot of free time reading -- well, erotica I guess you would call it. Ones where men are submissive and women are dominant."

"So it's something that's drawn you for a while."

Sue nodded as she curled her hands around the steaming mug. "I'm just not sure what to do now."

"We take some baby steps, find out a little more about where our desires lie. If you want to take this further than what we've already done."

Did she?

*Hell yes!*

"Okay, and if I said yes, what then?"

"What do you want to do? I'm willing to explore this with you, slowly of course. I don't want to rush you into anything and there will be a lot of things we have to look into. What we want to do, how we wish to take things, but if it's what you want -- well, it's what I want, no, what I need."

For a moment, Sue didn't trust herself to speak. It was one thing to dream about this type of thing, it was another to have a man offer her the chance to explore things further. And this wasn't just any man, he was her boss, so how was that supposed to work?

Her head threatened to start pounding.

"Why me? Why not go to a woman you pay so you know it's kept secret?"

"If all I wanted was someone to beat my ass, or make me lick boots on occasions then yes, I'd find a dominatrix to sport with. But I need more than that. I want the whole package. I want a woman who can be my wife, my partner, my lover, and who isn't afraid to be dominant with me in the bedroom, or beyond that if it's what we decide we both want."

"And you think that person, that partner, is me?"

"I don't know for certain. I want to say yes, that I know without a doubt that you and I are meant to be together. But nothing in life is certain, is it? I only know that I'm more comfortable with you than I've ever been with any other woman I've known before. There's something here, I can feel it, I just don't know where it will end up." He reached across the table, taking one of her hands in his. "But I want to try."

No declaration of love, or passion. No false words of hope. Just a soft smile that reflected in his eyes. The touch of his hand against hers. And something else. Honesty.

"I was expecting something else." She admitted, quietly.

"Ah, you mean something more along the lines of me stating I love you and I want to spend the rest of my life with you?"

Sue nodded.

"And are you disappointed that I didn't say that?"

"A little." What woman didn't want to hear that they were loved? "But we don't know each other that well, do we?"

"Enough to know that I care about you. No, it's more than that, but would you really believe it if I said that I loved you right now?

We've not spent that much time together…"

She blinked. Had she heard him correctly? Or was she just reading between the lines? "Alan? Are you saying that you love me?"

Alan fell silent, but kept hold of her hand, his brow furrowing.

"Or am I being foolish?"

"No, not foolish. I just  --  yes, I love you. I just wanted it to be special when I told you. Romantic even. Not in the middle of a discussion about dominance and submission at my kitchen table. Call me old-fashioned but I imagined something more, well, beach, moonlight, and a diamond ring." Alan gave a sheepish smile.

Romantic?

Didn't he understand what hearing those words, knowing that he truly did love her, care for her, want to be with her, meant? How she felt?

Tears stung in her eyes, threatening to spill down her cheeks.

He'd wanted it to be special, not just a series of words, an empty declaration, or something said just so he could tumble her into bed again.

"Sue, did I say something wrong?" He squeezed her fingers. "You look as if you're about to cry. God. Whatever it is, I'm sorry, please. I didn't mean to upset you."

"You didn't." Sue choked back the tears. How he could ever think she was a dominant when all she now wanted to do was cry, was beyond her. Female dominants were strong, haughty, they didn't care what their submissives felt, except on rare occasions, and they didn't cry like this.

Did they?

"Then what is it?"

"I thought you were just playing with me. It's just, no one's ever taken the time to think about what I might  --  how I'd like to hear those words the first time."

## Chapter Fifteen

Alan moved quickly around the table, wrapping his arms about her waist as he pulled her up out of the chair. "Oh love, I wasn't trying to hurt you. I'd never do that to you. I just didn't want it to sound as though I was saying something just because you needed to hear it."

Sue took a deep breath, trembling in his arms.

Did she think he was a jerk?

"Maybe you're mistaken about me?" She gulped the words.

"I'm not sure what you mean?" He brushed back the hair from her eyes. She was soft, vulnerable, and delicious all rolled into one. How could he be wrong about how he felt towards her? Maybe he should have found a better way to tell her of his feelings, or just blurted them out instead of sounding like a complete moron, but what was done, was done.

"I'm not a dominant. No Mistress would ever start sobbing the way I just did."

Is that what she was afraid of?

"How can you say that? A dominant is still human; do you think they just switch off everything?"

"Well, no, but nothing I've read ever suggested that they cry over things like this, or that they care about how their submissive, or slave, feels." She scuffed the back of one hand over her eyes.

"Oh love, sheesh. Ever thought that those books of yours wouldn't sell as well if the dominants ever showed a scrap of real human emotion? They're fantasy, not reality. Real people think, feel and yes, even cry, regardless of what type of relationship they are involved in."

"Are you sure?" Sue trembled under his touch, her breath coming in soft gasps as she slowly blinked the last of the tears free from her eyes. "I don't want you thinking that I'm something I'm not. It wouldn't be right, it just -- even if it bought us both a few months of fun together it would eventually break down and we'd hate each other."

"I could never hate you."

Sue pushed back from him, looking him straight in the eyes. "Yes, you could. If you love someone it's easy for that love to turn to hate if you feel as though you've been betrayed or lied to in some way. They're two sides of the same coin."

"I could dispute that."

Her lips quirked into a slight smile. "Are you disagreeing with your Mistress?"

He laughed, shaking his head. "And here I thought you wanted to take things slowly?"

"I do -- but --"

"And yes, I can disagree with someone even if I've submitted to them, just as long as I'm polite about it. Respect, manners, they're important. Even if you wanted to call me every name under the sun when we're playing, or I'm, erm, serving you, we'd keep that for our games only, not everyday use."

"I didn't know that."

The tears had passed, her nerves easing, or so it appeared to Alan. Her gaze narrowed then shifted as she glanced over at the clock on the wall. "Do we have time to talk about this now? I mean, we still have to do something about those men and the blogger ring."

"I think it's about time you showed me just what they are saying on that ring, don't you?" He nodded towards his computer in the small office room. "If you wouldn't mind showing me what you've found."

He'd taken a brief look over the pages, but he'd spent most of his time focusing on Sue. Perhaps too much time. He frowned slightly, only to smile as he shook his head and walked into the office. She was already acting like a dominant, getting him back on track. She might not know much about how a Mistress was supposed to act, but her instincts were there.

"Haven't you seen it for yourself?" Sue claimed the chair in front of the computer and booted it up.

"Just a quick glance."

Tiny lines tightened around the corners of her eyes and mouth. "If it was that important to you I would have thought you've had spent more time investigating it?"

Color and heat flushed across his cheeks. "I'm afraid I let myself get distracted by you."

"Hm, not good," she muttered, waiting for the screen to go through its loading warnings. "You might have missed something important."

He moved behind her and wrapped his arms about her shoulders, resting his chin on the top of her head. "You're important to me."

"And what these men are doing isn't?"

"No, I didn't say that."

"Alan, you help to run a business. Certain things can wait, the business and your responsibilities to it, can't. I would have understood, or even helped you." Tension flared across her shoulders and back.

"You're annoyed with me?"

"A little, yes. My hand's itching."

"Pardon?"

She turned a little, looking up at him as he was forced to lift his chin away from her head. "I have this sudden desire to -- well, to spank you and remind you what's important in life. Sorry. Maybe I'm getting into the idea of being a Mistress far too much."

"Part of being someone's dominant is correcting them if they forget things, or they misbehave. Or it can be if the two involved want that." He nodded towards the screen. "Okay, do you recall the address?"

Sue turned her full attention back to the computer, her fingers dancing over the keyboard as she tapped in the web address.

## *Curvaeous Heart*

"There."

The page loaded quickly and as Alan read down the screen his heart sank.

"Looks like they've been busy," Sue murmured, her voice little more than a whisper.

"Another date, another set of stats. And Victoria." The name threatened to stick in his throat. "There are details about her visit to the office."

"Who is she?" Sue's voice turned ice cold. "Naked under her coat, we all know what the boss was up to? What the fuck is going on? I thought you weren't seeing anyone?"

"I'm not!" How in hell's name had this *Dangerous Liaisons* known about Victoria? It had to have been someone who was in the building at the time, that much was obvious. But who would have seen her enter or guess that she was nearly naked under her coat?

His father had known about the visit and some of the details, but his own dad? Try to bring down the company? No, that didn't make sense. Alan dismissed the idea almost as quickly as it sprang to life.

"Then what was she doing in your office, half naked, if not fully naked. Just what do you think I am? Some sort of desperate fool?"

He took a step back from the chair, trying to read over her shoulder at the same time. "Sue, please, calm down. It wasn't like that."

"Then just what was it like? She was in your office the very same day that you asked me out! How could you!"

He opened his mouth, trying to speak. How could he explain to her what had happened? She wasn't going to believe him. He wouldn't have if the roles had been reversed.

"No excuses for me?" She crossed her arms under her breasts, staring at him. "Come on, tell me something. Some sweet little lie to make things all better between us? I'm sure you've pulled this with other women before."

"Do you really think that about me? That I'm the sort of man who would jump from one woman to the next?" His shoulders tightened, the muscles threatening to bunch. "Sue, I'm not like that. You know the lies they've been spreading on that site, and do you really think I'd take the risk of having sex with someone in my office when anyone might walk in? Please, think about this."

"You're the boss, you can stop people from walking in."

"Right, except for one thing. My father comes into the office on a regular basis. Ask around, everyone knows that. He'd been there once already during the day, so why would I risk being caught by my dad? Especially with all the shit that has been going on. Think for a minute, do I ever even normally date women at work, or hit on them?"

This wasn't happening.

How could she think he would do something like this to her?

*Because every other man she's been involved with has dumped on her in some way.*

"Everyone I've spoken to told me you didn't hit on women at work. Even that secretary of yours was bemoaning the fact you don't..." Sue's words tapered off.

*Good, think. Work this through, Sue. Please.*

She closed her eyes, stepping away from him as she frowned. "I need a minute. Please. I'll be back, I just need a little space right now."

"You're leaving?" Panic clawed at his throat.

"For a walk, I have to. I just need to clear my head."

He glanced towards the door then back at Sue. "All right, I'll wait for you here. But please, don't go home. I don't want you to storm off on me. I love you, Sue. Please, remember that. I really do love you."

# *Chapter Sixteen*

*Of all the stupid -- God -- why did I trust him? What was I thinking about? Was I truly just that desperate to get laid? No, please don't let it be like that. I thought – thought I was stronger, wiser. Oh God, what have I done.*

Sue closed the door behind her and headed down the path towards the gate. Her stomach rolled, knotting only to roll once more, leaving her struggling to keep from being sick. There were lies, secrets, things she couldn't have known when she'd first agreed to go out with him.

And now Alan's lies were out in the open.

*But I jumped into bed with him, not once, but twice. He didn't twist my arm in order to get me into this mess. I did this on my own!*

He'd given her the chance to say no, to stop it at any point she wanted to, she'd had the power.

So why hadn't he told her about Victoria or whatever the woman's name actually was?

Was he ashamed? She'd seen the reaction play across his face, the way he'd lost all color. If he'd been happy with whatever had happened in his office, then why would he react like that? It didn't make sense.

Then again, there were a lot of things that didn't make sense these days. Like actually being hit on without someone setting out to use her from the very beginning?

*That's it, put yourself down a little more, it's such an easy habit to fall into isn't it? I mean why bother to wait for someone else to do it when you can hurt yourself, right?*

No wonder it was always so easy to believe the worst about herself! She didn't need people like Bill attacking her, she did it to herself.

*So stop bemoaning the fact and stop it!*

"This isn't helping." She muttered and glanced back towards his home. In her anger she'd already walked far enough away from the house where she couldn't see the car.

The street was a nice enough one and it was obvious that the houses here belonged to families like Alan's, ones with enough money to feel comfortable. One or two car drives led down from each house towards a well-kept street. She doubted they ever had to wait for potholes to be fixed. No, with the taxes paid in this part of the town the local council would take care to make sure the residents had no room for complaints.

And he wanted her to share his life here.

Why would he even suggest that if he was busy dipping into Victoria and whoever else, it just didn't make sense.

Nor did his silence about the events listed on the blogger.

Had something happened that he had been ashamed of?

She stopped in her tracks.

Could it be that simple? He'd not mentioned it to her because he'd been ashamed? If he'd wanted the woman then he wouldn't have felt that way at all, so either she'd come in and done something he'd reacted to without thinking, or he was protecting the woman in question?

Sue turned back and looked at the house where she knew Alan would be waiting.

It was within his personality, or what she'd seen of it so far.

She wrapped her arms across her stomach. Had she reacted too quickly and not given him the chance to try and explain himself? Well, of course she had, any woman would have after being faced with a post like that on that damn blogger -- she wasn't made of stone.

*So you let something you know is done to make small-minded men feel better about themselves affect things between you and Alan. Smart move -- not.*

She was letting them win.

"Like hell I am." She scowled and began to walk back towards

## *Curvaeous Heart*

Alan's house. Whatever the men behind the blogger were trying to do she wasn't about to let them ruin what could turn out to be the best relationship she'd ever have the chance at.

Alan was a good man, so what if he'd made a mistake in not telling her about the situation, they were still practically strangers and they hadn't even met when it had happened.

Would he be relieved that she had returned? Maybe he wouldn't be expecting her to return? She had been angry. No she was still angry, but the focus of that fury had shifted.

She had no reason, no real reason, to blame Alan.

The men behind the hateful posts on the blogger were another matter entirely.

There was only one way to find out.

Sue rested her hand against the door then slowly pushed it open.

"Alan?"

Silence answered her for a moment. Had he left, gone to bed, was he in the back garden?

"Alan?" She took a step further into the house.

"I'm here, sorry I was..." He colored as he came into view, fastening his pants back up. "Bathroom, sorry."

She couldn't help but smile. He looked almost like a little boy caught doing something that he shouldn't.

"I didn't expect you to just sit and wait around for me, there's nothing to be sorry for."

"But there is, I should have told you about Victoria. If I'd been thinking things through I should have realized that, sooner or later, you'd hear about her visit and how she was dressed, or not as the case may be."

Sue nodded as she walked back into the living room and settled down on the couch. "So just what did happen?"

"She's been chasing me for a while and I've been keeping her at arm's length. That morning she got into my office, wearing a fur coat and little else. I was a little shocked, but unfortunately I'm also human so did react to her. She took that as a go ahead signal, unzipped me, and went down -- well, I won't lie. A part of me enjoyed it, but as soon as I had my senses back under control I put a stop to it and laughed her out of the room."

"So why has she been chasing you?"

"My father's idea. He's been trying to pair me off with someone for a while now. And Victoria's family is well off, she's attractive, at least in the modern, plastic, all fake and enhanced type of way, but she's not my type. Sorry, I like women who won't break the first time I...never mind."

She had a good idea what he was talking about and felt her own cheeks flame.

"I've had enough of being the focus of matchmakings, but Victoria has already been invited to the party on Friday and I've no doubt that she's going to try and get close to me. I was going to ask you if you'd like to attend it with me, but I'd understand if you didn't want to now."

"I'll need to think about it," she admitted.

"That I can understand. A lot has happened, and I don't want to push you away by acting stupid. You'll need time." He sat there with his head bowed slightly, his hands folded on his lap.

"It's not just time." Was it her imagination or did he actually look sheepish? "So you didn't tell me about Victoria because you didn't think to, or was it something else?"

"I thought if I didn't talk about it then maybe I could forget that it had happened. I'm not exactly proud of my reactions. It shouldn't have mattered what she was, or wasn't, wearing. It's just, well, I almost had no control. No, it wasn't that either. I did have control. I just didn't use it."

"So you think you did something wrong?" An idea formed slowly at the back of her mind. One that she hoped would show her clearly if he was lying about his desires or not.

"Well, yes, I guess I do."

"And you want that feeling to go away?"

His gaze narrowed. "Yes."

"And you claim you enjoy being submissive."

"I never actually came out and said that, but yes, I do. Or I think I do. Like you I don't have a lot of actual experience in this." A nervous tic twitched in his left cheek.

"Then maybe you need to explore it a little more, and I believe this might be the right time."

He paled, swallowing quickly. "Are you suggesting that I submit to being punished for this?"

"If you want to feel better, then yes."

"And what do you think I should do, then?" His voice dropped into a low whisper, a soft tremble working through his body. Was she imagining it, or was he looking at her with some measure of hope?

Had she hit on the right idea? One that would end the matter between them?

"How are submissives punished?" She wouldn't use the word slave, it didn't feel right. He wasn't her slave, her property, and she certainly wasn't a Mistress. She didn't know anywhere near enough to call herself that.

"It varies, ma'am." There it was, that shift in address, just enough to let her know that he did need to do this. "But I would think a spanking might be for the best."

Sue tried to remember what little she'd read about spankings. How they were done, what was said, or used during them to make the submissive feel -- well, submissive. She frowned slightly. Were there other phrases, terms, that she was supposed to learn? Ones that would describe the situation, how people felt, what she was meant to do, and why?

It just meant there were things she had to learn about, study and come to terms with. Especially if she wanted to be a part of Alan's life.

"A spanking. All right, then we'll go with that." Sue looked over the room. "Bring one of the kitchen chairs in here, and place it in the center of the room."

He flashed her a curious look then pushed to his feet and headed into the kitchen. Good, this would make it easier. Though she had to wonder why he hadn't insisted on a safe word.

*Why would he need one? This is a punishment, not a play session. And just a simple spanking. I can handle doing that, can't I?*

Alan carried the chair back in and set it down. "This is a punishment, correct?"

"Yes." Sue pushed easily to her feet, sliding out of her shoes.

"So you won't be looking at something that will turn into a play session?" He spoke calmly.

"Correct." Hm, he'd dropped the ma'am thing, okay. She could correct that as well.

"Then we won't need a safe word, that's all I needed to check. And for the punishment I submit myself into your care, ma'am."

Damn, he really meant that.

"Then we'd best get this over with. Strip, fully." She walked over to the chair, settling down as she planted both feet firmly on the floor. Hopefully the chair would take their combined weight.

He hesitated for a moment then nodded, pulling off his shirt even as he slipped out of his shoes. His pants and briefs followed moments later, his socks the last to hit the floor.

"Is that how you treat your clothes? Pick them up, fold them over the back of the sofa, then walk over to me."

He glanced back at his clothing. Was he going to protest? Would she have to add another punishment on top of this one just to keep some level of control?

She watched him, closely. Nude, athletic, sensual. Most men looked odd nude, almost silly, not Alan.

*No, focus on what you are supposed to be doing, not how good it would feel to have him back between your thighs, licking, kissing, suckling...*

She bit back a groan, barely suppressing a rock through her hips. No, this wasn't the right time, or place, for this.

## *Curvaeous Heart*

Alan nodded and picked his clothing back up from the floor, laying them over the back of the sofa just as she'd told him to. "Yes, ma'am."

Good, this was going slightly more easily than she had expected.

"Over my knee, put your hands on the floor, thighs spread, balancing yourself over my lap, boy." A soft shiver played through her body as she called him boy.

He flushed, lips parting in a protest that he swallowed quickly, refusing to give it life. Without another word he walked to the left-hand side of her chair.

Sue gasped as he laid himself across her lap. He wasn't hard. But the heat that came from him was undeniable. His naked back stretched out in front of her, his taut ass cheeks raised, waiting, ready for her touch.

What if she did something wrong?

She could hurt him and it would be too late to stop this, he'd never trust her again.

*Right, this is a simple spanking. How can you hurt a grown man from a spanking? Get a damn grip!*

Sue took a deep breath and traced her fingertips over the curve of his ass. He shook, lifting up into her touch. A soft whimper rising from his form.

Was he afraid?

"Trust me." She whispered.

"I do."

Good, that would make it easier.

"You've been a very naughty boy, haven't you Alan? You've been keeping secrets from me, when you should know better than to do that." She tried to keep her voice low, calm and focused.

"Yes, ma'am."

"So you need to be punished, don't you Alan?"

"Yes, ma'am. Please, punish me ma'am. I'm sorry I hurt you. I never meant to. I didn't think."

"Ah, yes. And there is the real reason you are going to be punished. Like a naughty boy you didn't think of what would happen; how I would feel. You were ashamed and hid it hoping it would never be discovered. Only this is a little more serious than catching you with your hand in the cookie jar, isn't it?" Sue lifted up her left hand only to bring it down, hard and fast on his buttocks.

He jerked across her thighs, head lifting with a soft cry. Heat blossomed across his ass cheeks, and burned into her hand. She hadn't expected it to hurt her as well. No one had mentioned that in the books.

Sue hissed and shook out her hand quickly.

"May I suggest, respectfully, that you cup your hand, ma'am. It won't hurt you as much, though it will also hurt me more." His voice shook as he spoke.

"Thank you, slut." Her inner walls quivered. Slut. She'd been called that more than once, but calling Alan that had unexpected results. This was punishment, it wasn't supposed to turn her on. But she couldn't deny the ripple of heat deep within.

*It's not the punishment, it's the power.*

That made sense.

She looked back down at his naked ass. The red had faded into a soft pink. Had the sting faded as well?

She cupped her hand, bringing it down onto his buttocks quickly. Once, twice, three times in rapid succession. He cried out, jerking across her thighs, his hips rocking forward. Not from pleasure, she could see that, but shock.

Sue shook out her hand again. It didn't hurt as badly but now she did understand why some parents used the 'this will hurt me more than it hurts you' routine. It did sting when you spanked someone. Especially someone as well toned as Alan was.

How many was she supposed to give? And wasn't he supposed to be counting them? Shit, she'd forgotten that part. Too late to bring it in now. She didn't want him to think that she had fucked everything up.

## Curvaeous Heart

Sue wracked her mind, trying to recall anything else she had read about spankings as punishment. Six of the best? Twelve. No, six would be enough this time. She didn't need her hand aching for several days to come. And they didn't always add in counting, but she could see where it would help sometimes.

Three more, she could do this. No, two, she'd given him one before being told to cup her hand. That wasn't so bad was it?

She lifted up her hand, pausing as she looked down at his pink bottom. He whimpered, shifting his weight across her lap, his thighs taut as he kept mostly in position. It had to be uncomfortable, stretched out over her lap, forced to hold position, to keep his balance like that.

Did he feel humiliated?

"Such a naughty little boy." She whispered, smiling as she saw him blush so hard and fast that it covered his back. "Maybe I should make you stand in the corner, with your nose to the wall, after this spanking."

He let out a low moan of fear. "Please ma'am, not that."

"You don't like the idea?" She brought her hand down without warning, harder than before.

"No, ma'am." He gasped, his head jerking upwards with the new blow. "Please, ma'am. Not the corner. I won't be selfish again. Please. I'll think of how things affect you. Forgive me, ma'am."

She'd never felt such a surge of energy as she did now. He was afraid, humble, pleading with her. Here he was, this man who could hire or fire her, who had the ability to make her feel alive, now without power, surrendering to her, begging for her forgiveness.

"Why should I?"

He gulped.

"Well, slut? Give me one good reason why I should believe you?"

"I don't have one, ma'am. I'm asking, no begging, for a chance, that's all. Please."

One last spank to give him, it wasn't that much and he didn't know for certain just how many she had decided to give him. But granting him a chance, forgiveness, that was another matter entirely. Did he deserve it?

She cared for him, loved him if she wanted to be honest about it, but if she was going to try and explore her dominant side then she needed to take that into consideration.

But what was the point in punishment if you then continued to beat someone up about what had happened? Punishment was to punish, to wipe the slate clean, and then give the punished one a chance to prove it wouldn't happen again.

Sue lifted her hand one last time, looking down over Alan's trembling form before she brought it down hard, and fast, onto his upturned ass. The crack rang out through the room, Alan's cry joining with the echoing smack as he jerked almost fully from her lap.

Her hand stung, even with cupping it, her palm now burned from the force of the blow. She took a long, slow breath, calming herself, focusing before she leaned down and whispered in his ear.

"I forgive you, Alan."

# *Chapter Seventeen*

His ass throbbed. Even new to the lifestyle, to being dominant, she'd managed to leave him with a sense of truly being punished. He hadn't cried, but it had been close, if she'd called him naughty one more time, or told him she was disappointed with him, then it would have been too much for him to handle.

How had she known what to do?

Not that it mattered now. The punishment was over and she'd given him a little time to calm down, wash up and settle himself before he walked back into the living room.

He leaned against the sink, focusing on his breathing.

Punishment. It wasn't supposed to arouse him, and when she had been spanking him he hadn't felt aroused, he'd been fighting not to cry, but now -- now his cock throbbed against his pants. His balls felt swollen, hot and heavy. Each time he closed his eyes he could feel it, her hand against his ass, the way she had traced soft lines over his back as he had trembled, trying to calm himself down, still laying over her thighs.

No, this wasn't the time for this.

Business. He had to focus on work, the blogger ring, the problems there, but his mind kept drifting back to Sue. The feel of her clothing against his balls, his cock throbbing as his hips pressed against her thigh. No, it hadn't happened that way. He hadn't reacted. He'd accepted the punishment for what it was.

But what if she spanked him again, for fun?

His balls tightened.

"Calm down, damn fool. Work, focus on work. We have those bastards to sort out. Sure, it would be good to crawl to her now, lick her feet and... shit I don't need this right now!" He ran the water, waiting until it was cold before he splashed some on his face. Maybe a cold shower would work?

Sure, until he looked at her, or thought about her again. She wasn't the sort of woman who you chased out of your mind with a mere cold shower.

Why though? They hadn't been together that long, and he'd never been in a position where a woman had invaded his being the way Sue had.

*Because I've finally found a woman I don't have to hide from. I can explore this, be myself, in all ways and she accepts me.*

How many women were there, out in the world, who would have accepted his desires? Or been willing to trust their instincts enough to push him into being punished in order to let him get past the problem?

*What problem?*

The one he'd known was there, but hadn't had the guts to admit to until she'd brought it up.

He glanced up at the small bathroom clock.

Time, always the enemy.

* * * * * *

Sue looked up as Alan walked into the living room and settled down on the couch. "There's a lot going on with the ring, the pressure to find them, to sort out the damage they've done has been growing ever since you brought the whole mess to my attention." He rubbed his temples and leaned back against a large cushion.

She frowned slightly, was he all right? He'd looked close to tears when she'd sent him off to wash up and dress again. Not that she could blame him. Spanking him, having him over her lap like that, had been emotional in a way she hadn't expected. Even now, as she looked at him, she could imagine him nude and kneeling at her feet.

"You've not been able to track them down yet? I would have thought you'd have put some people onto this, it can't be good to -- did you change the meeting by the way?" Bill, she knew the one in their office was Bill, but telling him would be a mistake. If he exposed everyone -- except it was going to happen sooner or later.

"Meeting?" Alan frowned then nodded, relaxing. "Yes I did, and it went off without a hitch."

"Good, they didn't manage to mess that up then." Sue relaxed a little more as she leaned back against the cushions.

"As for the blogger ring, I have a couple of ideas as to who might be involved, but getting the proof together is another matter. It would help if I knew who *Real Man* was. There are several mentions of him in the blogger being run by the creep in my side of the office."

"Mentions, in what way?" She hadn't read that far back in the entries in order to track it all down. Too many entries, not enough time and by the end of only a couple of hours both she and Barb had been dealing with both the need to throw up and a massive headache.

"The two men know each other, outside of the blogger that is."

A tight band wrapped around her heart. "So you think, if I can tell you who the one in my office is, then you'll be able to find out who the leak in your building is?"

Alan nodded. "I didn't bring you back here for this, though. I was hoping to talk to you about the situation fully at the coffee shop, but we had other ideas."

She blushed instantly. "Well, we both appeared to enjoy the change in plans."

Sue tried not to think of just how his body had looked when he had leaned over her lap, the curve of his ass, the feel of his cock and balls against her thighs. She'd darted into the kitchen when he had gone to wash off, but even splashing water on her face and hair hadn't helped that much. She still felt as if her cheeks were constantly burning.

"I've no arguments there." Alan chuckled and pushed the loose strands of hair back from his eyes. "However, I would like your help with this. I know you don't want to hurt anyone and I will do my best to keep your friends, and those at your work, from being hurt.

I don't want the women in my own employment upset either, but the longer this goes on the greater the chance that it will be too late to undo the damage. And at this rate whoever it is behind the leaks is close to ruining everything for my business."

Her stomach knotted. She tried to hide her discomfort by tucking her legs under her ass and pushing the damp hair back from her face. Small things that she hoped would prevent him from looking too deeply into her eyes.

"Sue, if you're not ready to help me on this I'll understand. I won't like it, but I'll understand."

"If I do agree to tell you what I know, all of what I know, then how will you protect the women involved?"

Alan closed his eyes, the lines deepening across his brow. "I have to press charges; you know that don't you?"

"Yes." She knew that only too well, it didn't mean she liked the idea though.

"So there's no way I can prevent these two men from bringing up the blogger, or the police from stumbling over it themselves, is there?"

"No, there isn't." She didn't like where this was going.

"Sue, if we don't stop them it's only going to get worse. The longer these men are left to get away with it the more women will end up hurt. Ones like your friends, and like you. Yes, I know you haven't been named on the blogger, except for a run in with *Real Man* the other..." He faltered.

The corridor incident. The color drained from her face.

"Bill, it's Bill isn't it. The one that's been targeting, teasing you?"

She nodded and chewed on the inside of her lip.

"Why didn't you tell me? You couldn't have thought that I'd laugh at you could you?"

"No, of course not. It's not me I'm worried about, Alan. It's always been the other women. One in particular. She works with me and I'm afraid her family will make her life a misery if this all comes to light." Ann, poor nervous Ann. She didn't deserve the sort of publicity that would come from all of this.

"Why would her family treat her so badly? I don't understand that. Family looks after each other; they don't lash out over things like this."

"Her brother is a cop and warned her not to get involved with men like Bill, she just -- she's afraid of what he will say."

Alan bristled, his hands clenched in his lap, tension playing openly across his shoulders. "Then either he's an asshole or she's letting her imagination get the better of her. I would think he'd be more interested in taking care of the wanker who hurt his sister instead of -- ah, she doesn't know for certain does she?"

"No, the last we spoke she hadn't told her brother yet and was still trying to work up the courage to go to him."

Alan fell silent.

Did she have the right to hold up everything based on one woman's fears? No, but neither did she have the right to dump all of this in Ann's lap. Ann had never said she couldn't tell people what was going on. Instead Ann had told her that she was afraid of her brother finding out. But what if Ann faced her brother with someone else at her side, a friend who would tell the man to shut up and think of his sister if he said something to upset Ann?

"I don't like the idea of waiting any longer, Sue. I can't hold up the investigation by keeping this information to myself. My father will be able to help track the man down, he's in and out of the office all the time, and he could have overheard something, or he might know if we had a Bill working with us at some point. Either way when I find out who it is, I can't wait for your friend to tell us it's all right to go ahead and do something about the man."

Standing by Ann's side might be enough to help the other woman, to get her to see that she wasn't alone and didn't need to hide in the shadows any longer, or at least hide in the small office.

"All right, I'm not happy with being rushed into this but I understand that we don't have another choice. If he's caught, if he's named, then will the damage be kept under control?"

"I don't know, it will be a close call, very close. But," he frowned, his voice trailing off for a moment as he drummed his fingers on his thigh. "If I can show Dexter that I'm capable of taking care of leaks, of following through with the information then maybe I can undo the damage. After all, it's not just happening in my office, but yours and other businesses as well. If we expose two of them, the rest of the ring might crumble."

She watched him through half-lidded eyes. Tiny lines crinkled at the corners of his eyes, emotions flashed over his face in rapid succession. The slight smile fading into a tight lipped grin, only to ease into a more comfortable grin by the end of it.

"When do you want me at the office?"

He blinked, staring at her. "What do you mean?"

"Well how else do you think you're going to be able to track him down unless I'm there? I know Bill, remember. I've seen some of the people he's met for a drink. Unfortunately he tends to use the same pub Barb and I go to on occasions. So I might have met this other man. Either way I'm not going to be able to help you whilst at my desk, unable to answer questions."

# *Chapter Eighteen*

Sue clutched the small box in her hand. She'd barely made it into work in time with her side trip to the store, but it had been worth the risk.

Hadn't it?

Barb had thought so, even if she didn't fully understand the meaning of the small gift. Then again she'd also enjoyed the look on Bill's face when Sue had been able to announce she'd be heading back out again shortly on the orders of their boss.

Did he know what was going to happen?

Sue replayed the look she had seen in Bill's eyes. Had there been any hint of fear? No, there had just been the normal piggish look of hunger and greed that she had come to know so very well.

"Are you sure he'll like that? It just seems a little odd to me." Barb leaned against the desk, her gaze narrowed on the fancy paper bag with its string of white and black ribbons. "Not the sort of thing I'd normally expect a man to like. You're going to have to explain the engraving to me at some point though."

"I will, just give me a few days. He's not the normal sort of man." No, he was one in million. He was someone who wanted her to reach into the depths of her heart and explore all of those naughty little desires with her. How was she supposed to tell Barb the meaning of the words she had asked the jeweler to engrave?

What would her friend say?

Well, there was no point thinking about it just yet. She had to see what Alan would say first. For all she knew he might not even want it, or be insulted by the thought of wearing it. She swallowed hard, a cold sweat threatening to coat her upper lip.

*No, don't think about that right now, there's enough to deal with, and he'll like it. He has to.*

"I've noticed that. It's just, well -- you know him best." Barb squeezed her shoulder and then glanced at the clock.

*I barely know him at all.* Panic clutched her heart. What if she was moving too fast, trying to push things too quickly? It could all backfire in her face and then what?

*At least this time I know what I want.*

"What time did he want you to meet him?"

"I'll have to head out in a few. Fortunately, meeting the boss at the other building is not the sort of thing I'm likely to be fired for." Sue pushed back from the desk and slipped the small bag into her purse. "I'll call you after this all goes down."

"You'd better. I'd give a month's worth of paychecks to be a fly on the wall."

* * * * * *

Sue. Another night with her, only to wake up with her in his arms. No sex, just a peaceful night sleeping with his arms wrapped about her shoulders, holding her close. They'd both needed that. Had it mattered that they had both had to work that morning? No, not really. At least she had made it to the other office building on time, even though he had been forced to run the gauntlet with Barb.

At least Sue had friends who could and would look out for her, and they'd have another night together all being well.

Unless something went seriously wrong.

*Such as? Face it, she loves you, you love her, what could go so wrong that she'd want nothing to do with me?*

He glanced up at the clock. It wouldn't be long before she'd arrive at this office and then maybe they'd get to the bottom of the matter with the leak.

"So what have you found out about the rumor mongers?" Neil Martin looked up from the couch in Alan's office. "And you could have at least answered the phone last night."

"Morning, Dad, good to see you too." Alan gave a brief smile. "I wasn't expecting to see you in my office this time in the morning. As for the phone, I had the ringer switched off. I didn't want to be disturbed."

"When Kevin Dexter calls me first thing to tell me the rumors have spread about the meeting this week and what are we going to do about the security leak then you can damn well bet I'm going to be in your office trying to find out what's going on."

Dexter? The senior partner of Harpers? Shit, this was not what he'd been expecting to deal with first thing in the morning. Sure, he'd planned on trying to find out a little more before his meeting with Sue later in the day, but this changed things.

"Fill me in." He hurried across the room and switched on his computer.

"It seems that someone in his senior management was sent an email, with a tip-off about the meeting. As they've been trying to keep the entire thing a secret he was less than happy about it being public information. He's got a couple of his backers about ready to pull out. Just as well you changed the date, it smoothed things over a little, but they're still very concerned."

"Not good." Alan frowned and settled in behind his computer. "All right, we know that the blogger ring is focused mainly on insulting women they know, or have had sex with, or both."

"Right." His father nodded. "You mentioned something about that the other day."

"I went back over the posts yesterday. There wasn't anything there about business matters until roughly the same time we started having issues. I've been trying to match some of the posts with the personnel roster and I've come across a couple of possibilities as to who *Dangerous Liaisons* might be."

"Dangerous who?"

"The name this particular blogger uses. But I've got someone coming who might be able to help. She already knows who one of the people behind the bloggers is. And she's willing to help me put the rest of the pieces together."

"Someone I know?"

Alan blinked and looked up. "Not directly, her name's Sue."

"Who?"

"The woman who I had the date with last night and, erm, the night before, she's also the one who brought me the information about the blogger ring."

His father frowned slightly. "And what makes you think she can help? She doesn't know anyone who works here does she?"

"Dad, just trust me on this. And yes, she does. She works in our other office. I was planning on bringing her to the party."

Neil laughed and shook his head. "Trust you? You've got nothing to go on. Hold on, are you telling me you went out on a date with someone who works for us? And you want to bring her in, as your date to a family and business function?"

"Yes, that's exactly what I'm saying. She's a very special woman and I happen to care a lot about her." *And if I told you the truth, that I love her, you'd have a fit.*

"Alan..."

"Dad, can we focus on the blogger ring right now and not my personal life?"

"Fine, but you haven't got enough to go on. There's no way you can track who these people are, not even if this Sue character has some hint of what's going on."

"I've got enough to make a good start, Dad," Alan tapped the keyboard. So many damn posts, and most of them made no sense. These were the ramblings of men that had been rejected or had managed to persuade a woman to get into bed with them, only to then what? Be dumped a few days later so they took their little petty issues to the online journals? If they were so brave, so sure of themselves, why didn't they use their real names?

That was it, cowardice. Of course, why hadn't he thought of this before?

The man he was looking for in their company would be a coward. It had to be someone who backed down to the other men around them, or tried to creep their way into power. Who did he know in the company that was like that?

"So, are you going to tell me about Sue? Or do I have to wait until she turns up? Do I know her outside of work? What's her family like? Have you checked into her background?"

Alan didn't bother looking up from the screen; he could well imagine the look on his father's face and had no intention of feeding into whatever mood his father was in. "She works in one of the departments over in the other building and came here to warn us about what was going on. Unless you're in the habit of mixing with secretaries, or their families then no, you don't know her."

"Are you calling me a snob?"

A slight smile tugged at the corners of his lips. "I'm just saying that you have some very definite tastes when it comes to company."

"Well, maybe you're right. So are you going to tell me about her?"

Alan flashed a quick smile. "Not right now, Dad."

"But you will be bringing her to the party on Friday?"

"Yes, if she'll come with me."

"And the reports, the ones we need for the meeting, are they ready yet?" His father switched track within a heartbeat.

"Charlie promised them to me for tomorrow, but I'm not holding my breath. If they aren't here on time, I'm going to fire him. Sorry Dad, I know he's been with the company a long time but I'm not willing to take that shit any longer."

"Charlie? He's been with us a while but he's not exactly been reliable for the past year or so now." Neil frowned, the slight catch in his voice enough to finally force Alan's attention away from the computer. "I stopped by his office on the way up here, it looked like it had been semi cleaned out. He was still there mind you, just his personal effects were gone and he was on his cell phone with someone called Bill. Are you sure he didn't think he'd already been let go? I can't see why else he would clean the place out like that unless he was getting ready to bail."

Charlie, Bill, the two men were alike from what little he knew about the man that had caused Sue so many problems at work.

The light switched on in the back of his mind. Could it really be that simple? Had the answer been in front of them all the time?

"Did he say much to this Bill?"

"No, but if it's the same Bill I've heard Charlie talk about before then they've been friends for a while. Those two are regulars at one of the pubs in walking distance from here. The Stag?"

"I know it." Most of those who worked in the building did. It wasn't the best of places, but it was easy staggering distance for both the main bus line and the local train station. Which made it a popular destination for the Friday after-work crowd, and the sort of bar Alan avoided like the plague.

"Dad, I've got an idea. I need to get hold of Sue. I think she might be able to help me with putting a stop to this." He couldn't wait for her to arrive, as they'd first arranged; if he was right this had to be dealt with now.

"And just why do you think she can help you?"

"Because if Charlie is talking to the same Bill that Sue knows, then we've found our link."

"And how are you going to prove it?"

"Sue. When she gets here she'll be able to tell us if she's met Charlie before." A face-on confrontation. If he called Charlie into the office with the report and had Sue waiting there -- yes, it could work. If Sue agreed. Was it fair to put her in the middle of this? She should be safe, he'd be here, and Charlie was a coward.

He glanced at the time. It was later than he had thought. There was no point in calling her over, as far as he could figure she'd already be on her way over.

"But in order to do that you need someone who can stand up and say, yes these two people are the same men and you think this Sue will be able to do that?"

"Yes." He looked up at his father. "I know she can. She's a strong woman, Dad. Very strong. And I think I'm in love with her."

"What? You've had what -- two dates with her? How can you possibly think that? You shouldn't be rushing into these things."

"Since when did it matter just how many dates I had with a woman before I knew what I felt towards them?"

"You're letting the stress get to you." Neil grumbled and leaned back on the couch. "However, I think I'll sit in on this little meeting. All of it. I'd like to see just what sort of woman has caught my son's attention."

Alan struggled against the urge to pace across the room. It didn't help that his father had insisted on staying put until Sue arrived, this wasn't exactly the way he had planned on the two of them meeting, but it couldn't be helped now.

"Are you sure she's coming?"

"Yes, Dad."

"Well, I don't like being kept waiting."

"She might have been caught in traffic. Give her a chance, Dad. Sue's a good woman." Not to mention attractive, intelligent, and the thought of her lying naked next to him in bed sent a wave of heat through his cock.

"And you know this from one meeting in the office and two quick dates?"

"It's been a little more than that." Shit, he hadn't meant to say that.

"You bagged her?"

"Dad!"

"Well you brought it up." Neil folded his arms across his chest. "So is she..."

"I'm not going to go into sexual details about my date with my damn father. I don't even do that with any of my friends. Sheesh, you and Mum raised me better than that, Dad."

Neil shrugged. "I did, but you can't blame me for trying. So she's hot then? Well at least you've got some taste. I was worried for a bit that you might find some skank to go out with just to piss me off.

You know the type of woman I mean."

"Dad. I'm not in the mood for this." He glanced towards the door. Maybe he could slip out, meet Sue and warn her?

"Well, it would be just the type of thing you'd try to pull on me. A way of getting back at me and your mother. Besides, I had someone try and tell me that you were out with a blimp of a woman who could have almost been old enough to be your mother."

Shit. This was certainly not going to make things easy when Sue arrived.

"When are you going to learn that I don't fall for stick insect women?" He needed to get something across to his father before things got out of hand. "I know you like women who look like fashion models, but I don't.

"That's just because you want to get back at me for interfering in your life. You know a woman like Victoria would be an ideal wife for you, and the children..."

"Dad, enough. We had this discussion already. I am not about to put up with you telling me who I should and shouldn't date. I'm not interested in a woman who I can't relax with, enjoy their company, their heart, mind, and soul. The type of women you try to team me up with are little more than pretty faces and empty hearts."

"Now that isn't exactly fair. Some of them are very nice women. I'd have loved to see you married to  -- oh what was her name. You went to school with her."

"Lynne? Shit Dad, I'm the wrong gender for Lynne. She's a die-hard lesbian."

"Now if you'd made a move when you had the chance then maybe she wouldn't be."

"Dad, it doesn't work that way. You can't change how someone's wired inside. It wouldn't have mattered if I'd dropped down on my knees and asked her to marry me every day for a year, Lynne is a lesbian. She's happily married to her partner now of three years and nothing's going to change that."

Why today, why now?

## Curvaeous Heart

Because his father wanted to push things when it suited him. Some things didn't change.

"So were they right, the woman you were out with is on the robust side?"

"She's a wonderful woman who I have a lot of respect towards. I enjoyed my evenings out with her." If it had been anyone else other than his dad there would have been an argument.

A sharp rap on the office door commanded the attention of both men in the room.

"Come in." Alan called out.

"Mr. Martin and, err, Mr. Martin, you asked me to escort Miss Night up the minute she arrived." Steph pushed the door open enough to let Sue in.

"Thank you, Steph. And Sue, please come in." Relief settled around his heart. Good, she hadn't let him down. Odd, for the most part he'd had no doubts, except for the ones his father had brought to life.

Sue nodded, the small lines around her eyes tight as she whispered a thanks to Steph and walked into the room.

"You need to talk to me, Alan?"

"Yes, but first I'd like to introduce you to my Dad. Mr. Neil Martin. My father."

Sue faltered, the color draining from her face only to flush back into both her cheeks. "Nice to meet you at last, Mr. Martin."

"My friends call me Neil. Mr. Martin was my father and he's been dead a good ten years now."

Sue ducked her head slightly. "Sorry."

"Nothing to be sorry about. Now please, as my son said, sit down. You're not on trial here."

She shot a quick look between the two men then hurried to the chair.

Great, his father had her terrified. She'd never talk to him again. Where was the strong woman he'd seen only the day before? Of course, she was meeting his father, who was also her employer, no wonder she was nervous.

"I must say I'm surprised. When my son told me the woman he had been out with last night could also help us with our little issue I hadn't expected -- even after the rumors I didn't think he'd go that far and go out with..."

"Dad, if you don't mind." Shit. Sue's jaw had clenched, her gaze narrowed, and there was a distinct glint in her gaze. "Sue, please excuse him. He's not been quite right since I turned down his last idea of whom I should date."

"Alan!"

"Are you going to let me talk to Sue, or are you going to find something else to make her feel uncomfortable?" He raised one eyebrow and fixed his father with a cool glare. "I asked her to come here to help us, not to deal with any shielded insults."

Neil frowned, his jaw tightening even as he spoke. "I'm sorry, she just caught me off guard. I had a different image in mind from what little you'd told me about her."

"I'm guessing you thought he'd be dating something young and slim." Sue's shoulders tensed.

Even from across the desk Alan could feel the ice in her words.

"Something like that, but I'm learning that my son isn't exactly predictable."

"Well, once we're done here I'll take myself back to work and away from your son so you can hook him up with something a little more to your liking." Her knuckles turned white as she spoke.

"Dad, Sue, can we deal with that side of things later. I did ask you here for some help, not to run the gauntlet from my Dad. And he doesn't decide who I go out with or who I fall in love with. So Dad, please, shut it. Unless you have something constructive to add to the conversation." He turned back to look at Sue, hoping she would hear the truth in his words. "Sue, I didn't ask you out last night to strike out at my Dad, or because I needed your help. I think I've made it pretty clear that I like the way you look. Shit, I more than like it. And if proving it to you means not finding out who's behind the leaks in my company, and letting the entire thing crash down around my ears then so be it."

Both Sue and Neil eyeballed him.

"No, I'm not out of my mind. I'm just not prepared to be told who I can and can't date any longer, either directly by you setting me up, Dad, or indirectly by you insulting the woman I love."

There it was. The L word.

"Did you just say you loved me?" Sue fixed him with a panic-stricken look. "In front of your dad? Alan, what on earth are you thinking about?"

"Yes, I did. And if you're not ready to hear the word in public then we can deal with that later, but the point remains the same. I need your help, but I won't let my father, or anyone else, insult you."

"I wasn't insulting her." Neil's voice rose and rapidly approached a shout.

"Yes, you were. You might not think you were, but I could see it, and it was obvious Sue felt the sting in your words. Now drop it, Dad."

Sue sucked in her bottom lip, trembling as her gaze flicked from one man to the next. Damn, he didn't like seeing her like this. Vulnerable. That was the only word his mind would link to what was going on. It took everything he had not to step around the desk and wrap his arms tightly about her.

Strength and vulnerability all in one woman, how could he be this lucky?

"Sue, if you want to leave, if you don't want to help us, I'll understand it." Sure, it would mean he'd have to call Dexter about the problems and call everything off on the deal, but it was better than letting his dad get away with treating Sue like that.

How many years had he dealt with his father trying to force situations? Either by direct orders or subtle manipulation? It ended. Now. Even if it meant walking out of the business and never looking back.

"I'm sorry, Miss Night." Neil spoke softly, a slight shake in his voice that Alan had never heard there before. "My son's right. Perhaps I've let a few blind spots get in the way of things. A couple of years ago I would have thought before opening my mouth, but I'm afraid the subject of dating has become something of a sore spot between Alan and myself. You got the brunt of that and it wasn't fair of me."

# *Chapter Nineteen*

"Alan, I want to say something to your Dad, but after we get this issue sorted out. The one you called me here for." Sue took a deep breath and tried to turn her attention away from the older man. How could someone be so cruel, and with no cause? Didn't he understand just how his words count lance into the heart of a woman?

Shit, she knew better than that. There would always be someone ready to call her a fatty, obese, wide-load, tubby, or something like that. There'd always be a newcomer who looked at her and never bothered to look beyond her body and some stupid ideal of what all women were supposed to look like according to a new fashion craze, or diet potion to sell.

"That's fine by me." His gaze narrowed for a moment, but that was it.

Good, whatever she wanted to say he wouldn't stop her. It might mean what was between them would come to an end, but if that was the case, so be it.

What was between them?

He'd said the word *love*. Had he meant it? Or was it something he'd just said to throw his father off guard?

"Hey, what if I don't want to sit here and listen to what your girlfriend of the moment wants to say to me?"

"Then I'll walk out with her. It's your choice, Dad."

A slight smile threatened to creep out of hiding. Good, he was ready to stand up for her. She wasn't sure if that was because of how he felt towards her, or because he was pissed at his dad. There was no real way of telling right now.

"So, what is it you want me to do?"

"I know this is asking a little much, but I think I know who it is that Bill has been talking to here, and I want to call him into the office to see if you recognize him."

"And what if he recognizes me?"

"Then, knowing Charlie, then he'll say something. Don't worry, I won't let him do anything to you, Sue."

She wasn't so worried about that. "Say I can identify him, what then?"

"I call the police and have him arrested."

"On what charges? I mean is he actually doing anything illegal?"

"That we'll have to leave to the police to decide upon. But I can call the police and have him escorted from the building if he doesn't agree to leave of his own volition. However, what he's done does come under the abuse of the Net. He's disclosed information without permission, despite the signed confidentiality agreement we have all of our employees sign and the way he's spoken about women on the Net, naming them, giving personal information. That might be covered by the anti-harassment laws."

Could it work that way? She wasn't a solicitor and had no clue about that side of things, but the chance to bring them down, to put a stop to all of this, was something she had to follow through.

"So, you're willing to try?" Alan smiled, that same heart-stopping glint in his eyes that she had seen a dozen times over in the past couple of days, but this time something snapped inside. "I know it's asking a lot of you, but..."

"Yes. For what little it might be worth, yes I am" How could she deny him when all she wanted to do was step around the desk and into his arms? It didn't matter that his father was there as well. Or that the older man didn't approve of her.

All right, so she wanted to do a little bit more than hug him. He did deserve a good spanking after the way he'd thrown her in at the deep end with his dad.

He gestured to one of the chairs then reached for the phone. "Then let's get this over and done with. I'll call him in and..."

"Wait, I want to say something first. Or rather ask you something."

One eyebrow shot up. "And what's that?"

"Remember the promise you made?" She met his gaze, trying to keep her breathing steady.

"Yes, I do."

"I'm calling that in now."

"Hold on a minute, I don't think this is the time or the place for whatever is going on between the two of you." Neil spoke up. "We've more important things to cope with."

"Dad, keep out of this, please." Alan didn't even look at his father. "Sue is important to me."

She glanced at the older man, then back to Alan. What if he didn't care for her, if it had all been nothing more than a way of getting her in bed? No, she knew he wasn't like that. She had to get her irrational fears under control. "I need to know something. I understand that this isn't really the right time to ask, but I don't think there will ever be a right time."

"You can ask me anything, Sue. No matter what. I made the promise. I'll keep it."

Sue took a slow, deep breath and looked him directly in the eyes. "Do you love me? Truly love me, they weren't just words you used to get what you wanted, or to shock your father? I need to know if you want, no, if you need me in your life."

"I knew it; she's trying to trap you into a marriage." Neil spluttered.

"Dad, please be quiet."

Her limbs trembled, heart racing as it threatened to pound free of her chest. Her palms felt sweaty. If he said no, then she knew it was just a fling, something they could both enjoy then move on when the time was right.

Which would be shortly after the blogger ring had been dealt with as far as she was concerned. It was one thing to enjoy his touch, but she cared for him, loved him, and the idea of him not returning those feelings....

Then she'd turn around, walk away and give up her interest in learning to be a dominant. It didn't matter that she'd finally realized she needed that, without Alan in her life it would be pointless.

"Yes, I do."

"Alan, you don't have to tell her that."

Had she heard him correctly?

"Dad, you taught me not to lie, not about things like this." Alan shrugged, his gaze never leaving her face. "And I do love her. I think I have since the moment she walked into the office a couple of days ago."

"But you've only known her for what, forty-eight hours?"

"And how long had you known Mum before you proposed?"

"That's not the same thing!" The older man stood up. "Things were different then, we knew what we wanted and didn't need to wait. She works for you, for us, and what do you know about her? You can't say it's anything like what happened between your mother and I."

"It's the same thing, no matter how you try to tell yourself otherwise. I know what I want, who I want to spend the rest of my life with and she's standing right here, Dad. You proposed to Mum only a twelve hours after meeting her. Well, I'm not proposing, I want to make sure Sue's happy before we even think about that, but I know she's the woman I love."

"Alan..."

"No, Dad, I love her, she's coming to the party with me if she wants to, and I'll be introducing her to Mum as my girlfriend."

Tears welled in her eyes, threatening to spill down her cheeks as she listened to Alan. Snakes knotted a dozen times over, only to finally begin to settle in the pit of her stomach, and still there was that soft voice of doubt trying to whisper to her that it was all a joke, a dream, a plot set up by someone to make her look foolish.

But the voice inside now lacked power.

The snakes no longer frightened her.

"Thank you." She looked at Neil, then back to Alan. So Mr. Martin Senior didn't approve of his son's choice. That was something they could deal with later, when the time was right. But for now they had other matters to take care of. One she was ready to face now that she knew the truth. "I believe I'm ready to take a look at this man for you."

She slipped her jacket off finally, setting it over the back of one of the chairs before she sat down, her gaze drawn for a moment to her purse and the small bag she had picked up before heading for work that morning.

Yes, she was ready for this, and everything that would follow.

The question was, would Alan be ready?

* * * * * *

Alan settled back in the chair, his gaze fixed not on Sue, or his father, but the door. Sue didn't move from the side of the desk, her back slightly turned to the door, but she'd still be able to see Charlie when he walked in.

Neil had fallen silent again, though the scowl he kept shooting Alan's way came as no surprise. Oh, his father would accept the situation in time, but until then there would be a few interesting days.

The party. That was going to be fun, especially if Victoria or some of the others were planning to attend. He could always ignore it, avoid the situation, except there would always be another party, another family event, or business get-together waiting around the corner. Still, he had every faith in Sue; the strength she had shown, even through her fear, had been far more than he had expected.

"Mr. Martin?" The door cracked open. "You wanted to see me?"

"Come in, Charlie." Had the man even changed his top in the past couple of days? Or did he keep a dozen identical tops in his wardrobe?

"I have the report you wanted, sorry its cutting things fine. I've been a little distracted recently. It will be done on time though."

Alan glanced at Sue briefly. Her shoulders had tensed, and she didn't look over at Charlie despite the fact that she wanted to.

"Come on in properly, Charlie. No point you standing at the doorway like that." Alan smiled and hoped he gave off some level of friendly appearance. He didn't need the man guessing what was going on just yet. Not until the right moment.

"I didn't realize you had someone else here." Charlie shifted his weight a little and nodded towards Neil Martin. "I didn't expect to see both of you here and..."

"The report?" Alan held out his hand. "I really need to go over it today, Charlie. You know we're pressed for time. You were told that it had to be ready, and I'm not minded to give you any more time to get it finished."

*Come on little fishy, come on in a little bit more where she can see you.*

"I meant to have this to you late last night, but I sort of got caught up with an old friend." Charlie smiled and walked in, offering the report.

Sue hissed under her breath. The sound barely audible but it was enough to catch the attention of both men.

"Shit!" Charlie took a step back. Panic flashed in his eyes, the color draining from his face. "What the fuck is going on here?"

"Something the matter, Charlie?"

"What's she doing here? She doesn't work in this building! She's not supposed to be here."

"Then you do know my guest after all?" Of course he did.

"I -- I've seen her around." Charlie's gaze flickered from one man to the next in the room as he backed up rapidly. The report still clutched in his hands, his knuckles white.

"We both know it's far more than that. It's time you came clean, Charlie. It will be better for you and your friends in the long run."

"You know? About the blogger, you know? I swear it wasn't my idea to take things this far."

"Sit down, Charlie." Alan rose and stepped slowly around the edge of the desk. "Yes, I know, and I know you're *Dangerous Liaisons* so you might as well just sit down and explain a few things to me. Like what made you think it was fine to try and smear the women you work with, or sell out my company for a few kicks. Did you get off on it? Did you like walking into work every day looking for some new piece of gossip you could post?"

"Oh God. You're going to fire me, aren't you? We weren't out to talk about work. You have to believe me. It wasn't like that. Not at first. It wasn't my idea to start that side of things. We were just keeping track of the women..."

"No, what was it like then? Did you one day wake up and decide, hey I'm going to be an asshole and destroy my job?"

"It was a game. Nothing but a game. But when I mentioned the idea of Bill sharing things that were going on at work we all thought why not, it added to the hits we were getting. The more hits the bigger the secrets we needed to keep the readers interested. The comments, the feedback, all those people coming to read our messages every day, it became addictive. Can't you see that?"

Addictive?

Even if he was telling the truth that still didn't excuse him. Anything could be addictive if you let it be.

"So it was Bill's idea?" His gaze narrowed on the trembling man.

"Mostly."

"Who else was involved?"

"Bill -- he swore me to secrecy on that. I can't. I'll lose everything. God, I just can't." What little color the other man had retained now drained from his face.

"Then you can tell that to the police. I'm pressing charges." So, there was someone else involved in all of this, but who was it? And how in hell's name was he going to find out?

"On -- on what grounds?" Charlie stammered. "I've done nothing illegal."

"Harassment, malicious rumors, I'll think of something. Oh I'm pretty sure what you've done is illegal, but I'm not a solicitor or a police officer. However, the police will be able to figure out just what it is you've done and what charges can be levied against you.

And I will follow them through. To the very bitter end."

"You can't do that to me! I haven't done anything that deserves that. Fire me, yes, but not that. Jail? For a few posts on the Net? It doesn't make sense. It was just a bit of harmless fun." The file fell from Charlie's hand, papers scattering across the floor. "Mr. Martin, you can't do this to me, we were just having a bit of fun."

"If it had just been a bit of fun then why did you nearly cost this company thousands of pounds? Why have you been hiding your words under an anonymous name? And why if it was just a bit of fun are you having problems telling me just who else Bill is working with?"

Charlie opened his mouth to protest then closed it again, shaking his head.

One piece of the puzzle left to work out, to find the answer to. They'd come this far, worked out the details, it wouldn't be long before he had the rest of the information and then the ring would be shut down for good.

"A bit of fun doesn't need the protection you took care to use, does it? I'm sorry Charlie, you and your friends did it to yourselves. And I strongly suggest you tell the police everything you can about just who else is involved in this fiasco. It might be the only way you can prevent them from prosecuting you to the full extent of the law."

# Chapter Twenty

"I'm so proud of you." Alan closed the door behind him, locking the world out as they both kicked off their shoes in his living room. "You didn't lose your cool, not even with the shit my dad pulled on you. Which I am sorry for. He had no right to talk to you that way."

"Some people don't think before opening their mouths."

"And some like to sit in the background, like whoever it is that persuaded Bill and Charlie to take things one step too far on that damn blogger. It's just a pity they wouldn't tell us who was behind it."

"Give it time, we'll find out who else is involved."

"Of that I have no doubt. Somehow, with you at my side, I feel as though I can take on the world."

That's what she needed to hear.

Sue walked fully into the room before she turned to face him. "Thank you, I wasn't sure if I'd be able to go through with it. But then I remembered that I had nothing to fear. I had the power, not them. Just as I do with you."

She watched as he blinked, staring at her. "What do you mean?"

"You're submissive to me."

"Yes, but I haven't submitted to you."

"Yet." She tried not to smile.

"That might take some time."

"No, I don't think so, Alan. You see you want to submit to me, we just need to decide if we're both ready to do this, knowing we're going to be learning along the way, that we will make mistakes, and that we'll both end up apologizing to each other for them." She hadn't removed her coat and now slipped her hand into the pocket, pulling out the small red paper bag.

"Sue, are you sure about this?"

"Is it what you want?"

"Well, yes. It's just that everything I've read about this says we should wait." He frowned, looking at the bag. "It's not that I don't want to submit to you, but I don't want to rush into this either."

"I'm not asking you to fully submit to me, Alan. I'm asking you take a consideration collar from me." Had she remembered the term correctly? She'd done a little research on the various types of collars that could exist in a D/s relationship, and this one had sounded ideal.

"Do you know what one is?" Alan peered at the bag.

Her jaw clenched and she took a slow breath, trying to calm down. He wasn't attacking her, he was questioning. Okay, that she could handle.

"Yes, I do. Alan, please sit down for a minute." She nodded towards the couch.

Alan slipped off his coat and settled down, not on the couch itself, but the floor. "Perhaps you should sit down as well then?" He tapped the cushions above his head.

Alan at her feet?

A soft shiver ran through her body at the thought of it, and before she could change her mind Sue curled up on the sofa above him, her coat tossed over the back. This felt right, on so many levels that she couldn't even begin to describe it.

"I'm not questioning your idea, Sue. I just need to know what you think a consideration collar is. In case -- well, in case I've heard something different."

A polite way of saying that he wasn't sure if she'd done the research or not, or had been deceived by someone online.

"As I understand it a dominant offers a collar of consideration to a submissive as a mark of intention, or desire, to look into a further relationship with the submissive. It's something beyond casual dates, conversation, or play. It marks to the two involved, and others that we're forming a potentially serious relationship." Sue frowned, she'd had all this memorized but now it sounded cold. "I want you in my life, Alan. You've said you want me in your life."

"I do."

"And you want to explore being submissive to me, correct?"

"Yes, I do." Alan leaned against her legs. "More than anything I've wanted before."

"A consideration collar allows us to do that. It's not you submitting to me, it's an agreement between the two of us to explore this." She reached down, running her fingers through his hair. This felt so right, Alan sitting at her feet. He belonged there.

"You looked this up?"

"Yes, a place called Steel Dawn." Had she remembered the name of the site? She'd looked over so many in the last day or so that some of them were little more than a blur in her memory.

Alan nodded, falling silent as he remained leaning against her legs.

Was he going to refuse her offer? Her other hand clenched around the small bag. Had she gone too far in buying this, getting it ready in the few hours she had been able to steal that morning? Maybe he'd ask for more time before entering into this type of arrangement.

Just as long as he didn't turn down the idea fully.

"You've thought about this a lot then?"

"Ever since you submitted to me for that spanking." Her belly tightened at the memory. "You've taught me something about myself. I do have a need to be dominant, but I've also learned something else. I don't want to dominate just anyone, it's you I want to own, to guide and to learn with."

Alan shifted away from her legs, turning around until he faced her. Without a word he slowly moved onto his knees, tucking his heels under his ass, his back straight, shoulders rolling until he lifted his chin up, looking her directly in the eyes.

"I know we both have a lot to learn, ma'am, but I would be honored to learn more about my desires, this need to submit, with you."

"Then you're willing to accept a collar of consideration from me?" Her heart threatened to lodge in her throat.

"Yes, I am."

Sue's hand shook, though she tried to keep her nerves under control. "I bought something for you, in case you decided to do this with me. I just hope you'll accept it from me."

His gaze flickered to the bag in her hands then lifted back up to her face. There was a soft tremble in his voice as he spoke, tears glimmered in his eyes, threatening to spill down his cheeks. "Ma'am, I would be honored to accept any gift you'd choose to bestow on me, but knowing this is to mark our entrance into this world together, it would mean all the more."

Sue opened the bag, pulling out the heavy silver bracelet. Solid links with a small space for engraving. "I hope this works in the place of a collar. I wanted something you could wear that wouldn't look out of place on you."

His eyes lit up.

"I had them engrave it with *Sue's Alan.*" She'd spent so long trying to figure out just what she could have them put on the bracelet. "I wanted something that said you were mine, if you accepted this, but nothing that would cause problems for you at work."

He nodded, swallowing hard. His voice choked, barely more than a whisper. "I don't know what to say."

"Yes, or no, it's all I need to hear."

His smile almost split his face. "Yes. Yes, a thousand times, yes."

"Your hand." Why was it so hard not to cry right now? There was a lump in her throat, one that threatened to close off her ability to speak. "Which wrist do you want to wear this on?"

Alan lifted up his left wrist.

Silently she fastened the bracelet about his wrist, fumbling with the clasp as both of them trembled. Her fingers didn't want to work and what should have been a simple operation took close to five minutes before she finally managed to fasten it on his wrist.

"Thank you, ma'am." His eyes glittered. "I don't have the words for what this means to me."

Neither did she.

Slowly she slipped off the couch, resting her hands on his chest. Heat blossomed between her thighs, her sex aching with the need for his touch, but there was something else, a need to dominate, to take control, to lead him into a sweaty, burning cry of passion.

It was just a step, a small one, and one of many to come, but they'd take it together.

He nodded, leaning back as he uncurled his legs from kneeling and settled back onto his left hip.

"Don't move, unless I tell you to."

"Yes, ma'am." His cock thickened beneath his pants, a low groan forming at the back of his throat as Sue leaned down and slowly unbuttoned his shirt. It wouldn't be easy to strip him without his assistance, but she could always order him to move just enough to help her.

His shoes, just like hers, had already been kicked off. It was one less thing to worry about.

She slipped her hands under the now open shirt, teasing her fingers across his chest, his nipples small, tight, hard little buds under her caress. Sue sucked her bottom lip into her mouth, her own nipples puckered, pressing against her bra cups as she looked down at Alan. Did he know just how much this meant to her? His trust? His love?

She traced a long, slow path down his belly, watching him shiver beneath her touch. His lips parted in a soft whimper, his hips rolling long before she undid his belt, sliding it free of his pants.

"Please," he moaned.

"Stay still, don't move remember? You wouldn't want this to end up with a spanking and then with you forced to stand in the corner of the room, unable to touch me whilst I played with myself." She leaned down, letting her fingers brush lightly over the throbbing outline of his cock, her lips capturing one small nipple for little more than a heartbeat.

"Evil woman." He gasped, arching up into her touch.

"Yes, and you love me for it." She grabbed his erection through his pants, squeezing gently.

Alan almost arched up from the floor.

"Careful, I could almost come right now, ma'am."

"But you won't. You won't come until I give you permission, will you." Her grasp tightened just a little more on his cock.

"No, ma'am. I won't." His eyes burned with a hunger he struggled to control.

Sue nodded and released her grip. She'd never known a man who desired her as much as Alan did. There was nothing hidden in his gaze, no deceit in how he acted towards her, he truly did want her, not just as a girlfriend, or an easy lay, but in all ways. She only had to look at the bracelet now fastened about his wrist to push away any doubts.

She blinked back the tears that threatened to cloud her vision.

Her fingers closed on his zipper, but even that light touch was enough to send a fresh shiver of delight through his body. Did he wonder what she would do next, if she'd even allow him permission to come when the time was right?

Tempting thought, but he hadn't done anything wrong and that would be a punishment. Besides, with what she had in mind it would be impossible for him not to come sooner or later.

Slowly but surely she slipped his pants down around his hips, pushing them to his thighs, then lower, leaning closer as she eased them along. Heat radiated from his groin, his cock still trapped beneath his briefs, his thighs teased by the soft touches of her hair. He wanted more, she knew that even without his speaking.

"Watch me," she whispered as she stood up and took a stepped back from him. "I don't want you to take your eyes off me."

"Yes, ma'am."

She nodded, looking down at him as she began to unbutton her blouse, sliding it slowly from her shoulders until it pooled about her ankles on the floor. He groaned, watching her as she traced her breasts through the bra, teasing her fingers over her nipples until she felt them throb, aching for his touch, his lips, his tongue playing over her coral tips.

It would have been so very easy to tell him to get up, finish stripping her and make love to her until she passed out, but she needed to take control, keep control, and learn just how far she could rule her own body.

*To be a master you must first master yourself, so the same must ring true for a Mistress, even one taking their first steps into this lifestyle. If I am to be everything he needs me to be, everything I know I want to be, then I have to stay in control.*

She slid her fingers down her waist, scooting them into the band of her jeans. "Do you want to see more, my slut?"

"Yes, ma'am. Please, yes!" His hands clenched into tight fists. His pulse throbbed in his temples, hips lifting from the floor as he struggled to keep control of his body. His cock surged against his briefs, a small damp spot growing across the head of his taut erection.

"How much more?" She traced the tip of her tongue over her lips.

"All of it, please ma'am. I want to see all of you."

"And what if I stop?"

He groaned, closing his eyes for a moment before he forced them open once more. "It would be your choice, ma'am."

Butterflies swirled around her stomach. Her choice. Would she ever get used to that idea?

Yes, in time she would.

Sue edged her feet apart, slipping her pants down her thighs before she stepped out of them slowly. Could he see the damp patch on her panties, or feel the heat she knew now radiated from her sex? Even if he didn't she knew he sensed it, hungered for her, but he would watch, wait, and hope that she would be merciful.

And for that, if nothing else, she loved him.

"Maybe I should just straddle you now, you with your briefs on, me in my underwear, and ride you. I know I could come that way."

She licked slowly over her lips. "You, on the other hand, wouldn't be allowed to. Perhaps that would bring it home to you just who is in charge?"

Alan shuddered, his hips rolling, back arched as he struggled to keep control of his willful body. "Ma'am, have mercy, please. You're in charge, your will rules here."

Restraints, she needed to buy restraints.

She hooked her thumbs in her panties, sliding them slowly down her legs, knowing full well his gaze was now locked on her exposed mons. How far could she take it before it was too much? Before his hunger took control of his body and they both regretted it?

*Not being honest, what about my hunger? I need him just as much as he needs me.*

He groaned as she walked over to him, wearing just her bra, and straddled him. One foot on either side of his hips.

Her inner walls rippled, her appetite gnawed its way upwards from her feet, setting her nerve endings on edge, threatening to burn into her core. Teasing him, touching him, it had all added to her own hunger, and now she looked down on Alan like a woman who had been denied food for days.

Just a little more, she could push this further, she had to. She had the strength, even though she wanted to strip him down and feel his thick cock press her tight walls apart.

She moaned softly, rolling her hips, tracing her hands down over her belly before one delved between her thighs, parting her sex lips for a brief moment.

That was all it took.

Alan cried out in despair and lust combined. His cock straining against his briefs, struggling to find a way free as he was left clawing at the floor beneath him. "Ma'am. Please!"

She lowered down onto her knees, straddling him fully, her sex so close to his now. Without another word she tugged his briefs down just enough to let his shaft free, suppressing a soft moan herself when it sprang, erect and throbbing, against her pussy. She rocked against it, not letting him slip within her hungry walls, teasing her clit on his shaft.

The smooth skin rubbed over her tiny nub, urging her on with each slow roll of her hips. Cream coated her lower lips, ready, willing, and eager to take him deep within, but she'd surrendered herself to the slow, sensual dance across his hips, their shared hunger teased into a ravenous need.

With a low groan she lifted up just enough to feel the head of his cock now slide over her labia and pressed one hand against his chest. His heartbeat vibrated through his body, rapid, hungry, matching the glaze in his eyes.

"Now?" she whispered.

"Now," he pleaded.

He cried out, arching his hips as she eased down onto his thick cock, taking it an inch at a time into her heated core. Her walls shuddered in a long spasm about his erection, her breath catching in the back of her throat once she settled down fully across his hips, resting her ass back on his thighs. For a moment neither of them moved, each content for the moment to ride the waves of delight that they now endured.

She took a slow breath, looking down at him. This is where she belonged, with Alan at her feet, under her body, his focus on her pleasure, their shared life together. She wouldn't allow that power to go to her head, no, she made that promise to herself now. She'd never become one of the heartless, cold women she had read about and had, for a time, wanted to be. Now she knew there was something more to being a dominant, even a new one.

There was love.

And there was Alan.

There was the desire they shared, the need to control and be controlled. Their mutual dreams of dominance, submission, pleasure, and perhaps pain.

What else did she need?

She groaned, her hips dancing slowly on his cock.

"Please ma'am. I want to see all of you." His words came in a series of quick gasps, sweat building across his brow and chest.

Sue nodded, her thighs tensing as she balanced herself fully. Her eyes locked with his as she moved her hands behind her back, slowly unhooking her bra. Her nipples ached with the need to be touched, they throbbed and stood out as crinkled coral pips on her soft breasts. She waited, holding the bra in place, her hands locked behind her back, arched, daring him to touch, to break the rules, to rip the bra from her body.

He groaned beneath her, hips rolling, each sensual sway pressed his cock against her walls, urging her to move with him. Her thighs tensed, her belly grew taut, each breath slipped free from her body with a low moan of delight and still she needed more.

She shuddered, arching, lifting half off his cock as she struggled to regain control of her body. She wanted to give into the pace he set, to surrender to the bliss he offered, but it wasn't time. She had to keep control here. He trusted her to remain in charge of not just him, but her own body, to show him that she would guide him deeper into the realms of pleasure.

Slowly, her arms trembling, she slid her bra away from her breasts, baring them to his view as he let out a long, slow, hungry moan of sheer pleasure.

"So full and delicious."

She crossed her hands over her breasts, covering them. "You forgot a word."

"Ma'am," he whimpered.

"That's right, and who commands here?" She pressed down fully onto his cock, her walls fluttering, closing, only to release.

"You do, ma'am." His thighs tensed. "You do."

"And who do you belong to?" She rolled her hips, first one way, then the other, dancing on his eager erection.

"You, ma'am, always you." His shoulders tensed, upper arms bunching, hands clawing at the floor beneath him.

"You want to touch me don't you?" God, how she wanted his

touch as well. Her hips rolled, claimed by a need of their own, she couldn't stop the long, slow rock on his cock, or the way her walls rippled, clenched, only to ripple again. Her breath burned in her lungs, belly tightening, a quiver claiming her thighs.

How much longer could she hold out?

For as long as she had to.

"Yes, please ma'am. Let me touch you." Alan groaned, half sitting up only to then struggle and force his body to obey as he laid back down again.

She traced her fingers over her nipples, pinching them lightly, each soft touch burning into her core. Molten heat coated her inner walls as she rode on a wave of pleasure, pressure and pain. Each breath took her closer to the edge, to the abyss until she no longer knew if she could hold on, control it, or if it would come up and swallow her whole.

"Please. Have mercy, ma'am." The muscles in his neck corded. "I need you. I need to come. I can't hold it any longer."

Sue groaned, leaning down, her hands clawing down his chest. "Come for me, slut. Come and scream for me."

Alan cried out, arching up from the floor as he wrapped his arms about her waist, burying his head between her breasts. She should have told him no, pulled away from him, punished him for touching her without consent, but she wanted this as much as he did now. She needed it with every fiber of her being. Her inner walls rippled, every nerve ending struggled to find a way free of her control and surrender to the delight that threatened to swamp her senses.

"Yes!" Alan screamed into her breasts, his cock throbbing, swelling against her inner walls until she felt it, heat coating her already molten walls. He shuddered arching up into her, his hips rolling to meet each rock of her willing body.

She couldn't hold back any longer, nor did she want to.

Sue sobbed, wrapping her arms tightly about his body, her nails digging into his back as her thighs tightened fully. Thought fled, emotion, sensation, that's all she now knew, understood and accepted. Her hips rolled one last time as the pressure spiked through her body.

"Mine!" she screamed, her nails tasting his blood.

"Yours ma'am, always yours."

*Always ...*

# *Chapter Twenty-One*

Charlie's words kept repeating themselves in the back of her mind. Bill's response had been the same, or so Barb had told her -- she'd been there when the police had collected him from the office and had reported the entire scene back to Sue the first chance there had been.

*Just a bit of fun, they hadn't meant any harm.*

So it was fun, was it, to ruin people's lives. To make fun of them? And what about the third party involved, there was still no sign of either man being willing to hand over that name.

"Sue, it's going to be fine. You're with me." Alan reached out and cupped her chin for a moment, brushing his thumb across her cheek.

Black tie, black pants, matching black shirt, her fingers itched with the desire to strip the clothing from him and remind herself just what lay beneath. Was going to the party so important? The past two days had almost been a blur, rushing from one thing to the next as they'd tried to tidy up the mess left behind by Bill and his friends.

That was the one thing she regretted, not being there to see Bill arrested at work, but perhaps it had been for the best? She might have lost control of herself and lashed out, but what good would that have done?

If anything else it could have backfired and given Bill a way of fighting some of the charges that even now were being levied against him. Charlie had been another matter. Apart from a few small comments when she'd bumped into him in the pub with Bill, he'd not actually done her any personal harm. Nothing more than the snarky comments she'd dealt with through most of her life.

It hadn't been personal with Charlie.

Bill -- with that man it had never been anything other than a personal attack on every woman he had ever come into contact with.

"We could stay here and just have a quiet night to ourselves." She reached out to tug at the tie he wore. It would have been so very easy to pull it free from his neck and start on the buttons. "There's still some paperwork to go over, about the blogger ring."

"Nothing that can't wait. The police will get the ISP to cooperate and we'll have the rest of the names within a few weeks at most."

"I just don't think I'm ready for this." Sue avoided looking at him.

"If we don't go to this one then we'll never make it to the next. There will be other excuses, other reasons we come up with to stay home together and they'll assume that they've won."

"Won?"

"That we're afraid of them. They'll start the whole rumor that we know we're not supposed to be together, or that we're not going to make it as a couple, or that I'm ashamed of you, or some other petty little excuse that fits their mood."

She looked over at the door, then back at Alan. Hiding behind the closed doors, she'd done that for far too many years as it was. All those people who were too ready to judge her based on what?

Their insecurities?

No, she wasn't going to play that game any longer.

"All right, then let's do this before I change my mind, again." One night out, followed by what? Something more intimate? A slight smile tugged at the corners of her lips. They'd barely had chance to sit down for a coffee since everything had broken loose at work.

He looked good in his fancy suit and tie, she couldn't deny that, and the dress he had paid for ... she'd never owned anything so sensual and daring. Sue smoothed her hands down the soft midnight blue dress with its laces that cinched in her waist. Even with the extra pounds she carried, one thing Sue had always been proud of was the fact she did have a waist.

So it wasn't as tiny as the models' on a catwalk, but she no longer cared. Alan loved her for who and what she was, not some fake image that had been plastered across the magazines.

"You look beautiful." Alan curled his arm about her waist. "I'm the luckiest man in the world and tonight I'm going to show you off."

His father would be there, and who else? His mother, obviously, a woman she'd not met yet, and she's already heard rumors that Victoria, the woman she knew had tried to seduce Alan in his own office, would be at the party.

*Come on, you faced down Bill, then Neil, what could be so hard about meeting a woman Alan's already turned down?*

Just nerves, with Alan at her side she'd be able to face anything, including this so-called ideal woman. Oh, she'd heard the descriptions of Victoria, how she had a perfect 10 figure, and could have any man she wanted.

She glanced over at Alan, a smile claiming her lips.

*Almost any man.*

* * * * * *

Despite all his words to Sue, facing his family and assorted friends wasn't quite as easy as he wanted it to be. She wasn't the only one they'd be judging, it was just that he'd become too used to being sized up at these events.

So why hadn't he told Sue?

*Because she has enough to deal with right now. I'm not going to add to the fears I know are there.*

"Do you think your dad will at least be polite today?" Sue closed the car door behind her and slipped her arm into his as they stood in front of the large house. A dozen cars were parked in the wide driveway, lights shone from the windows, and even from here they could hear the hum of life.

"Yes, with my mother around he wouldn't dare be anything else but polite. She won't let him forget if he disappoints her publicly."

"It sounds as though your mum is the one in charge." Sue's voice trembled. "I shouldn't be afraid; this is just a party after all."

"Yes, it is, but it's one where you have to face my dad again and then the unknown quantity of my mum and everyone else there at the party. I'd be nervous too if I were in your shoes." He shifted his arm, slipping it about her waist instead as he held her close. "But we'll be fine. Trust me."

With his arm still wrapped tightly about her waist, Alan led the way through the parked cars to the front door. Even though he lived in his own place he still couldn't help but think of the house as home. Until now.

The door opened up easily enough, unlocked with the constant coming and going of guests, each one well known to his parents. It was just a case of walking into the house and facing the crowds.

"I'm right here with you, Alan." She leaned in and whispered against his ear. "It's just a party, remember?"

His lips twitched into a full smile. "Turning my words against me just isn't fair."

"I'm not blonde."

He chuckled and led the way into the wide entrance hall.

The swell of people swallowed them instantly. Just how many people had been invited this time? More than he had been expecting. Instead of being able to find his parents quickly, it took Alan and Sue almost half an hour before they finally tracked them down.

"Alan, I was wondering when you'd finally show up." His father called out as they walked into the kitchen. The older man's gaze flickered to Sue for a moment, his jaw tightening before he turned his attention fully back to his son. "Good to see you could make it. You're looking well now that all that nasty business at work is taken care of."

"There are still a few pieces of the puzzle to work out through."

From the large walk-in cupboard his mother appeared, her hair immaculate as always as she set down the spare glasses. "Alan, darling. It's good to see you. Your father wasn't sure you'd be able to make it tonight."

"I told him we'd be here."

That caught her attention fully, and she turned her gaze on Sue. For a moment his mother didn't speak as she looked Sue slowly up and down, then a smile shone in the older woman's eyes, the tiny lines about her lips and eyes tightening as she walked across the kitchen.

"You must be Sue. It's good to finally meet you. I seem to have heard a lot about you in these past few days." Margaret Martin reached out and took hold of Sue's hands, pulling her a step away from Alan.

"Nice to meet you also, Mrs. Martin." Sue managed to smile, though she was well aware of the tension that now played across her shoulders. His fingers itched with the need to reach for those knots and work them out of her body.

"Please, call me Margaret, or Maggie if you're comfortable with that. I get the feeling you and I have a lot to talk about." His mother finally spoke again, her gaze flickering towards Alan's wrist before she focused her gaze back on Sue. "Perhaps we can find a quiet place to talk?"

Alan's heart dropped into the pit of his stomach. "Mum, we've only just got here. I don't think we should be..."

"Alan, I don't believe I mentioned including you in the conversation between Sue and I, did I?"

He knew that tone all too well. "No, Mum."

"In that case, Sue will you come with me? We've got a lot to discuss."

"Maggie, I'd like to stay with Alan for a while."

"I understand you're a little nervous, but I'm not my husband. I don't go around judging the women my son dates based on silly things like fashion. No, I'm already aware that you've made my son a very happy man, but there are a few things I'd like to discuss with you, including the gift you gave Alan."

Alan paled and found himself stuffing his hand into his pocket before he was even aware of it.

"There's no reason to hide it, Alan. I think it's a perfectly sweet gift but I'm sure you understand why I would want to have a quiet chat with your *lady*, don't you?" A merry glint danced within his mother's eyes, her lips twitched into a knowing smile.

God. Had he been right? Did his mother know about that sort of thing?

"I think that it might be a good idea after all. Alan, we won't be long. Would you mind hanging my coat up then? And getting some drinks ready?"

"Yes, of course." Alan nodded, taking her coat. "Are you sure about this?"

"She is, Alan. And I think your father has something he wants to say to you as well, don't you dear?"

Neil paled, swallowed hard and then nodded. "Yes, of course. Your mother is right, we do need to have a quiet chat, my boy."

The last thing he wanted to do was spend time having a private conversation with his father, but Alan was also very well aware that his mother wasn't about to be argued with.

"Sue?"

"I'll be back soon." Tiny lines tightened around the corners of her eyes. Her jaw had clenched, but her eyes glinted with sheer determination. "Trust me."

"Always."

* * * * * *

"I'm sure you're a little concerned about why I wanted to talk to you." Margaret closed the door behind them once they were safely in the large bedroom. "First I'd like to apologize for my husband's behavior towards you."

Sue froze in her tracks. "You know about that?"

"Neil and I have no secrets between us. He told me and he's been punished for his behavior. He knows very well that..."

## *Curvaeous Heart*

"Punished?" Sue's gaze narrowed on the older woman, Margaret settled herself down into a high back chair. Had she heard correctly? "Did you just say punished?"

"Yes, which is something I am sure you're going to learn a lot about with my son. Part of the duties of a Mistress include correcting behavior when there is a call for it."

Sue felt the color drain from her face. "I think I need to sit down."

"Feel free to. I doubt you were expecting the conversation to take this twist, and you've every reason to be a little unsettled right now." Margaret nodded towards the second chair in the bedroom. "I realize this is a lot to take in, but once I realized the type of relationship you and my son shared, I knew that we would need to have a short chat. No doubt one of many to come."

"You know about -- oh God."

"Take a deep breath and calm down. It's not that bad. I had a similar discussion with Neil's mother not long after we were married, though of course things were a little more difficult then. There weren't so many sources of information available, and now of course you have the Net, which I have no doubt you'll use on a regular basis."

"I think I need a drink."

"You'll be fine. And I've long since known that my son needed a strong woman in his life. Not just the type that would walk over him, but a woman who understands the difference between bullying and dominating. There aren't that many men, or women, who are able to walk that line. Oh I know the sort of women my husband kept pushing at Alan, they just weren't suitable. Not when it came down to it."

Sue was still trying to wrap her thoughts around the idea that Margaret Martin knew about dominance and submission, and that they were actually having this conversation.

"Are you telling me that you and Mr. Martin have a D/s relationship?"

"Yes." Margaret leaned back in her chair. "And I've been waiting for the day that Alan would bring home a woman with the strength to take that role in his life. I just hope you realize what you're taking on. Being someone's dominant is not easy."

Sue forced her thoughts into some semblance of order before she dared to reply. "I'm new to all of this."

"Which can be both a blessing and a curse, but from the gift you've given my son I understand you two have taken a step into a formal relationship?"

"A consideration collar." Sue nervously licked her lips. "I'm sorry, it's just that having this conversation with you feels a little  --  well -- odd."

"I imagine it would be." Margaret smiled. "A consideration collar? Now that's not something I've heard of in a long time. It used to be a common thing amongst the old community."

"Community? There are others locally who?"

"Yes, there are. And a few of them now bring either their daughters, or their daughter-in-laws. Still, the majority of the group is around my age. There are far more male dominants than there are female ones, which is a shame. Still, I'm sure there are others who just aren't aware of our small group. You are, of course, welcome to attend our next little get-together."

Others?

Women like her who needed to be in charge of their relationship?

It wasn't just some sick little fantasy she'd indulged in?

Of course it wasn't. Her short search on the Net, and a quick visit to a well-stocked alternative bookstore had proven that, but to know there were others who lived locally that she could turn to for advice was a different matter entirely.

"Does Alan know about all this?"

"No, he doesn't. He might be more than a little surprised to know that at least one of the women there has a vested interest in him. But she's just not suitable for my son. She's far too willing to cross the line between consent and abuse. Oh, not physically, but emotionally, mentally, and those can be just as damaging. I'm hoping that the commitment you and my son have made will be enough to finally tell her that she needs to back off and leave him alone."

"Are there really those who cross the line? I thought that was just something put on sites to frighten people, or it just existed on the Net."

"No, they do exist. Men and women, submissive and dominant who don't care who they hurt just as long as it means they get what they want."

Her mouth dried out. "So what happens if she doesn't take the hint?"

"Then she'll be blackballed. If she doesn't leave Alan alone then I'm sure you and I can handle the matter." Margaret smiled slightly. "But if she has any sense, she will leave him alone once it becomes clear that you and he have taken this first step. A consideration collar is not something to be disrespected."

That, at least, was good news.

"Where do these meetings take place?"

"In our homes. Formal tea parties you might call them. Those of us with trained submissives sometimes bring our boys with us to tend to the service. It's all very relaxed for the most part. I don't tend to bring Neil with me though; he doesn't always play well with others, as I am sure you've noticed. He prefers to keep his submission to me private."

Sue nodded, a part of that made sense. Men like Neil wouldn't want others knowing about their desires in case others took it as a form of weakness. She'd read through more than one essay on that recently. "I don't think I could bring Alan either, especially with you there, it might be uncomfortable for him."

Uncomfortable didn't even begin to describe it. How could she ask him to act in a publicly submissive manner? He wasn't ready for that.

*No, let's be honest here. I'm not ready for that. I don't know how*

*Alan would react to the idea, but I'm not sure I could handle it.*

"Which would, in turn, make it difficult for you. Being a dominant doesn't mean forcing your submissive into situations which could be detrimental to their family relationship. Although I've always known he was a submissive looking for the right dominant, I don't believe I'd be that comfortable with the idea of my own son wearing a collar and a frilly apron, serving me tea and scones at the next event."

Sue couldn't help but laugh at the thought. "No, bringing him to that sort of get-together wouldn't be a good idea."

"Because of his reaction?" Margaret's gaze narrowed.

"No, because of mine."

Tension seeped from the older woman's body. "If you're willing to admit that failing then you truly are the woman my son needs."

# *Chapter Twenty-Two*

Neil Martin led the way into the small office after stopping by with his son in the living room. It was enough to buy them both time to have a private chat without one of his guests coming in search of them

"Alan, I'm sorry. Your mum made it very clear, I had no right to treat Sue the way I did." Neil Martin pulled out a chair from behind the heavy oak desk and sat down. "I just let myself get caught up in the hope that you would find the type of woman that I -- well it's your life and from what your mum has said I might have missed a few things about Sue when I first met her."

"She's a good woman and I love her. That should be all that matters, Dad."

His father didn't look up from the table. "Yes, it is. It should have been. I can't do anything more right now than tell you I'm sorry. I just hope that's enough."

It would have to be. What else could he expect his father to do?

"She's a very special woman."

"I hope so. I don't want to see you hurt. I was just a little con-cerned. She's a touch on the old side to have children with. It's something your mother and I always wanted, grandchildren."

"There's always adopting, if we decide we want children. And women are having babies into their fifties now."

"Not safe though is it?" His dad shrugged. "Not that it's any of my concern. I just hoped -- ah, never mind what I hoped for."

Children, his father's expectations, is this what it had all boiled down to? The hopes of a would-be grandfather? Still, this wasn't the time, nor place, for this conversation. They had guests to tend to, business matters, and when Sue returned he had every plan on introducing her to each person at the party. If nothing else it would show Sue how much he loved her, and confirm to others just how important she was to him. A way of putting an end to the rumors and husband-seekers who wanted to find a way to sink their claws into the money they assumed he had access to.

"So, do we sit here waiting for them to return or --"

"Alan, I was wondering where you were hiding. Someone mentioned they'd seen you arrive." Victoria's voice cut off the rest of his words.

Alan tensed and turned to face the imposing young woman. "Hello, Victoria. I wasn't sure you'd be here tonight after our last meeting."

"Your father invited me several weeks ago, and I'm sure if I was no longer welcome then either he, or your mother, would have informed me that the plans had been altered."

Victoria. She hadn't changed. Any other woman would have been ashamed of the way he had sent her packing. She had left the office half naked beneath a fur coat, a spurned lover instead of a triumphant woman. Now she stood in the doorway, dressed in the height of fashion. A long cocktail dress of deepest red, split to the hip on one side, drew further attention to the figure she was well used to flaunting when the need arose.

"We didn't exactly part on the best of terms the last time we saw each other. I would have thought that would have been enough of a reason to stay away tonight."

"Well, I decided to forgive you for that mistake and give you one last chance. After all, we both know you had other things on your mind that day. I should have taken that into consideration." She walked smoothly into the room closing the door, her lips gleaming from a faint coating of well-applied lipstick.

"And just what things might those have been?" His gaze narrowed. He wasn't in the mood to deal with Victoria and her insistent need to try and be a part of his life.

"Approaching you at work was a little foolish, I should have arranged to meet you elsewhere, away from the stress of everyday life." Victoria walked around the table, tracking one hand over his shoulders then down his arm before she turned her attention, briefly, to Neil. "Evening Neil, if you don't mind, I'd like to speak to Alan alone."

Alan felt his hands tighten into fists. His skin crawled under her touch. Odd, once it would have set his body aflame, but now he wanted nothing to do with her.

"Actually I believe I'll stay. The last time I checked this was my home, not yours, Victoria." Neil met her gaze calmly. "And you are a guest in my home, but that does not give you the right to request me to leave. I suggest you remember that in future."

"In that case, Alan, I believe we should move elsewhere to continue our conversation."

"No, if you have something to say to me you can do so in front of my father."

"Alan, I don't believe that would be a wise idea. This is something of a delicate matter." She pouted slightly, turning to rest her right hand fully on his shoulder. "I'm sure you can appreciate the need for privacy with such things. If nothing else your little problem at work should have made that very clear."

"My little problem?" Had she overheard something during her brief visit to the office? Or realized what was going on when the secretary had escorted her through the building?

Neil's gaze hardened instantly but he kept silent this time.

"Oh, come on now Alan. It's common knowledge. The blogger ring, company secrets all over the Net. Perhaps if you had a real woman in your life, one with business sense, you'd be able to keep a firm hand on your company." Victoria leaned in close, brushing her lips along his neck. "That's what you need, a woman who knows what she wants and isn't afraid to go after it."

His stomach knotted. "Victoria, if you had any idea just what had been going on at work then you'd keep your mouth shut."

"And if you don't learn to treat me with a little more respect then I will make sure that your recent little problems will only be the tip of the iceberg compared to what you will be doing next. I tried to warn you, I don't like being pushed to one side. I get what I want, and I want you."

"I'm not some prize up for grabs." If she'd been a man he'd have been ready to throw a punch, but hitting a woman, no matter how angry she managed to make him, just wasn't a step he was willing to take.

"No, you're not a prize, not in the sense that most people would think. You're handsome enough but that isn't the reason I'm interested in you. Neither does it have anything to do with that nice little business you and your father run. No, it was the long chats with your mother that finally made it clear to me that I had to step in and take charge of the situation."

His mother? What the fuck did his mother have to do with this?

"You're a man, one I want. And I don't take well to being told no." She leaned in, nibbling at his earlobe. "There's so much I can show you, teach you about yourself, but the first thing you need to learn is not to tell me no. I won't tolerate it."

"Get used to hearing it from me, Victoria." He growled, pulling away from her touch. "I'm not interested in you and if I have to hire a skywriter and proclaim it in mile-high letters in order for you to understand then..."

Victoria's gaze narrowed on the bracelet he wore, her fingers closing about the silver links as she used her hold on it to drag it further into view. "What the fuck is this?"

"A gift from the woman I love and plan to marry." He yanked his wrist back.

"You bastard! You're going to toss me over for someone else? Who is it? That tart you came here with? Oh don't lie to me, Alan. I told you I knew you'd arrived. More than a few people are talking about that overweight frump you turned up with. She's what, nearly old enough to be your mother, isn't she? If you think I'm just going to sit back and let you settle with that bitch, then you truly don't understand the lengths a woman in love will go to."

"You're not in love with me, Victoria."

"Oh yes I am, and unlike your overweight little pet I do know what love is."

"You'll leave Sue out of this. I don't care what you or others might think, I love her, fully. She's all I've ever wanted or needed in a woman."

"Take it off now. You're mine. You've always been mine. I've had you dancing on the end of my strings for the past month, you were just too dumb to realize it." Victoria snarled, her normally pretty face twisted, her eyes darkening. "I've worked my way into every facet of your life but one and that becomes mine tonight. If you try and deny me I'll do a lot more this time than start spreading rumors that you're gay."

Cold sweat coated his top lip. He didn't like where this was going. Or what his gut was telling him. "And just what do you think you can do to me, Victoria?"

"I can make sure that every little secret that didn't make it up onto the blogger suddenly becomes public knowledge."

"Charlie and Bill made it clear they were working with someone else, but they were both too afraid to give me the name. Thank you for clearing that up."

"Oh, don't pull that one with me, Alan. You're nothing but a silly little submissive male who needs a strong hand to tell him what to do, and that's me. I've trained for this, spent my entire life studying, preparing for the day when I would finally have my own little boy toy, so imagine my surprise when I found out that dear Margaret's son was a submissive male just waiting for the right woman to come along."

A cold hand clamped about his heart. "What did you just say?"

His mother? No, his mother would never have encouraged Victoria to come after him like this.

"Oh, didn't she tell you? Your mother's known for some time. She doesn't like me though, told me to stay away from you, but what's she going to do to stop me? You can't even stop me. Not really. Not when you're fighting the urge to come and kneel at my feet even now. Oh don't try to deny it. I saw it in your eyes in your office. You wanted what I was doing, you needed to give into that, but something wasn't quite right for you. Perhaps I wasn't forceful enough at that moment. That's when I realized that you're the type that denies what you are, you need to give into the idea that you're being forced, manipulated, even blackmailed. Just like those silly little money sluts. The ones that spend all their money on women they never even meet, phone goddesses who control their lives and wallets."

"I'm nothing like that."

"Oh yes you are, you're just hiding it, Alan."

His jaw clenched, every muscle in his body tensed, and still his father kept silent. This wasn't happening, all the problems at work, the constant stress, it couldn't have been because of one woman who refused to accept that no meant no.

"My son isn't a piece of meat to be grabbed by the hungriest predator." Neil finally spoke up.

"No, he's a submissive male who needs the strongest woman around to keep him in line and that is me."

"Stop and think for a minute, do you truly believe what you're doing is the action of a dominant?" Neil stepped around the edge of the desk.

"I believe I know far more about being a dominant than you or your son ever will. You're both submissive men, and in your case a poorly trained one. I would have thought better of Margaret considering how everyone else in the group looks up to her, but it's obvious that she's only been playing at being your Mistress all these years."

"Haven't you learned anything from the women around you, from those in the lifestyle? Strong doesn't mean abusive. Abuse is not a part of a good D/s relationship. The reason my wife makes such a good dominant is she knows where the line is. Where the limits are..."

"You stupid little fool, there are no limits unless a dominant wishes there to be." Victoria hissed and turned to Alan. "You belong to me and it's time you accepted that."

Alan shuddered as he caught a glimpse of the fanatical light that shone in Victoria's eyes. Dangerous. Why hadn't he seen it before?

Because he hadn't looked, she simply hadn't interested him enough to peer beneath the surface he'd seen prior to tonight. No, that wasn't entirely true, he'd kept her at arm's length for a reason.

This woman, this creature, expected him to go along with her desires and if he didn't then what? She'd cause more problems for his business? He couldn't allow that. He wouldn't bow down to her either. The thought of her touch left his skin crawling in sheer disgust. This wasn't the woman he wanted, or needed.

"The only thing I'm going to accept is that you need help, Victoria. You've been playing games with people's lives and I'm not going to tolerate that any longer."

"You're mine Alan, and you have two choices. Accept that of your own free will or I'll force you to your knees kicking and screaming all the way." Victoria closed the gap between them, her hand tangling in his tie, tightening the noose of silk about his throat in a single move.

"And I suggest you get your damn hands off my property before I lose my temper." Sue's voice broke through the rapidly gathering fog of anger and fear that now threatened to cloud his mind.

# *Chapter Twenty-Three*

Sue waited only long enough for Margaret to enter the small office before she closed the door and turned her attention fully to the woman who now had a tight grip on Alan's tie.

Her stomach knotted as she took in the scene. Alan caught by the tie she had straightened before they had arrived at the party, his jaw clenched, shoulders tight. If Victoria had been a man she had no doubt Alan would have already fought his way free of the unwanted grip. But he respected females and now those lessons prevented him from slugging the woman.

"Your property? God, I never thought he'd stoop so low. Do you even know what it means to be a Mistress?" Victoria's grip never loosened from the tie. "He'd be with me if he had the ability to choose freely. We both know that. It's why you gave him that damn bracelet, so he couldn't make that choice."

"From where I'm standing I'd say I have a better understanding than you ever will." Sue forced her voice to remain calm, despite the fact that her heart pounded against her rib cage loud enough that she was certain everyone in the room could hear it.

*Get off him before I rip your fucking throat out.*

That's what she wanted to scream at Victoria, but it wouldn't have helped the situation.

"Margaret…"

"Neil, be silent and stay out of this." Margaret interrupted him with a sharp wave of her hand. "This is between Sue and Victoria."

"Yes, ma'am." The older man lowered his gaze.

"He's mine, Victoria. He and I have agreed to a consideration collar."

"He had no right to accept such a thing from you. He belongs with me. What sort of Mistress are you going to be; you can't even control your body. Look at yourself. You're fat!"

## *Curvaeous Heart*

The words should have hurt, and only a week ago they might have left her shaking, trying to control the urge to cry, but now Sue saw them for what they were. They were nothing more than the weapons of the insecure, petty words with no real power behind them unless she, Sue, allowed them to affect her.

"Did you have anything else you wanted to say, Victoria? Or did you want to continue with the childish insults?" Sue folded her arms beneath her breasts. "I didn't think a woman could be involved with those idiots on the blogger ring, but now that I've seen how you act it makes sense. You're no better than they are. Lashing out, trying to control everyone around you. Using force when you don't get your own way. What's next, blackmail?"

Victoria blinked, her grip on Alan's tie slipping.

"Alan, come over here please."

Alan nodded, taking a slow breath as he walked away from the shaking Victoria.

"Listen to you, some dominant you are. Asking your toy to do something instead of telling him. A Mistress commands, she doesn't ask. We control, we demand, if I wanted him on his knees I'd tell him, not ask. You're weak!"

"I'm stronger than you will ever know."

"Prove it. Command him, show your strength, your power over him. You can't can you. It's just some bedroom game to you. A way of getting off, or have you switched roles already? You've let him tie you up, didn't you?"

"If I was a switch I wouldn't be ashamed of saying so."

"You're weak. I know what Bill used to say to you, and you'd let him walk all over you."

"Yes, for a time I did. Then I stood up to him. He didn't know what to do then. You see, like most bullies, he was and still is a coward. Just as you are."

"Haven't you learned anything about this lifestyle, Victoria?" She almost felt sorry for the other woman. She wasn't a dominant, but rather a bully, alone and afraid of the world around her. How often had she seen men and women like this? People who had to lash out, control, use acts of cowardice and cruelty to get their own way? Hadn't she fallen victim to men just like Victoria on more than one occasion?

"A dominant is just that, a dominant. They don't make bargains, or ask their toys to do something." Victoria's jaw set.

Sue shook her head, her anger seeping away. "No, they use what is appropriate to the situation within the limits of their submissive."

"The only limits that matter are those of the Mistress. Submissives are there to obey, to please. What they want doesn't matter." Victoria's eyes glittered, her hands clenched into fists at her sides.

"You're confusing D/s with abuse. And if that is truly what you believe being a dominant is then you'll quickly find yourself in prison for assault. Alan and I have a long way to go in this lifestyle, a lot to learn about each other, but the one thing I know now. I'd walk away from him in a heartbeat if I crossed that line into abuse."

"A submissive wants a strong Mistress, someone they know will take charge of the situation, not a weak-willed little bitch like you. Alan needs me. He knows that. He's just too afraid to make the right choice."

"Do you believe that Victoria? Do you truly believe that?"

"Yes."

"Then there's a simple answer, isn't there. We give Alan a free choice."

"Do you really think I'd fall for that? He knows it's not a free choice, he's wearing your collar -- bracelet."

Sue held out her hand to Alan. "Alan, I need you to give me the bracelet back."

"But..." Alan began.

"No, give it back to me Alan. It's important you have free choice, fully free choice in this." She closed her fingers on the bracelet as he placed it in her hand. Her heart sank into the pit of her stomach as she held the silver links tightly. No, she had to keep her emotions under control in case Victoria accused her of using them to manipulate Alan.

"You're a fool."

"Perhaps, but I prefer to give him a true choice." Sue took a deep breath and looked at Alan. "No matter who you decide to be with I want you to know that I will support your decision. If you want to kneel at Victoria's feet, then I'll be the first to congratulate her and wish you joy in your new life."

Oh, it hurt to say that. Each word stabbed into her heart like a rusty knife.

Alan didn't move.

"Alan, darling. You know which of us is the right choice for you." Victoria purred, turning to face him fully.

Sue stood her ground, though her heart threatened to sink into the depths and never return. It didn't matter that she knew Alan loved her, right now all she could see was the beautiful body of a woman who knew that she could attract the attention of any man she wanted with little more than a twitch of her hips.

Victoria was everything a man could want. Young, attractive, and wealthy, and that is what men needed in a woman. Not a woman who was middle-aged, overweight, and worked as what, a secretary? What did he see in her to begin with?

Sweat coated Sue's palms as she stood there waiting, and still Alan didn't move.

"Come now, it's not as if it's a difficult decision is it? She has nothing to offer you, at least I will be accepted by your friends and family." Victoria glanced towards Margaret and then laughed, shaking her head. "Well, your friends at least. What good would you gain by keeping that little bitch in your life? She has nothing to offer you, she doesn't even know how to feed that needful fire you've finally admitted burns in your heart."

"There's no choice to make," Alan glanced towards Sue then turned the full force of his attention on Victoria. "I've known for a long time that the type of woman that I want in my life, the type of woman I need, possesses a rare strength. That she goes after what she wants, despite the knowledge that others might ridicule her for it. Women -- no, not just women, but people with that level of courage are all too rare."

Sue closed her eyes, struggling to keep her fears under control. He wasn't going to choose her. Why would he? He was right, that type of courage was rare and she barely had the courage to look into the mirror some days. How could she have ever thought she would be enough for him?

She'd told him he was free to make his own choice and even though it was about to bite her in the arse she had to follow through with those words.

"Ma'am, will you have me in your life, at your feet?"

Her heart skipped a beat even as she opened her eyes.

Alan.

He knelt at her feet, looking up at her.

Her mouth dried out as she wiped her hands on her dress.

"Alan, you have no idea the mistake you've just made."

"Oh shut up, Victoria. You still haven't learned have you, even after all these years. You can't force someone into doing something they truly don't want to do. And my son has made his choice. He wants Sue. I suggest you learn to live with it." Margaret's cool voice cut through the room.

"Though not for too long. I plan on pressing charges against you for your part in the blogger ring." Neil spoke quietly, but his voice never wavered. "My apologies, Margaret, I know you told me to keep out of this for now, but it is a business matter as well."

"Understood."

Sue didn't move as she stood there, looking down at Alan still kneeling at her feet. The others faded into the background even though a part of her registered that Victoria had somehow been involved with Bill and Charlie.

"Ma'am, will you have me? I know it's a lot to ask but I want to be with you. I need you in a way I never knew was possible. All

## Curvaeous Heart

I ask if that you accept me for everything that I am, the good and the bad, and give me a chance to be at your feet, in your life, and in your heart."

She tried to force her mouth to work but all she could do was nod. Tears clogged her throat, stinging in her eyes as she grasped his hands and half pulled him to his feet. The small nagging voice of doubt she had lived with throughout her life now whispered at the back of her mind that there was something wrong with him kneeling at her feet in front of his parents, but she no longer cared.

She had Alan.

Nothing else mattered.

# *Epilogue*

Alan shuddered under her lips, his limbs outstretched on the bed, bound by scarves. His hips raised towards her, a low groan filling the air. Sweat coated his skin even as she shifted over his body, teasing the head of his cock with her slick lower lips.

Her breath burned in the back of her throat, hunger rippling through her belly and into her thighs as she danced slowly across his throbbing shaft, never quite letting him slide into her body. She ruled here, owned him, controlled him, and only she would set the pace.

He strained against the soft restraints, his hands clenched, jaw set. It wouldn't have taken much effort to pull free, just a few sharp tugs, or a single word and he would have been able to wrap his arms about her body and turn the tables on her.

But he didn't.

He wouldn't.

This is what they wanted, needed, and craved.

Victoria. His parents. The business. None of it mattered right now. There would be other days to deal with the fallout from the party.

Here. Now. This bed. His cock. Her control. That's all that mattered.

Slick heat coated her sex. Her clit throbbed and she eased one hand down over her belly, easing her lower lips apart to brush her thumb over the heated little nub of flesh. His eyes lit up, the tip of his tongue traced his lips, wetting them softly.

"Please ma'am." He moaned, lifting his hips higher off the bed, desperate to find a way to bury his cock into her tight, heated walls. "I need you."

"Who do you belong to?" She leaned forward, pressing her cream-coated fingers against his lips, sliding them in until he tasted her heat, suckling on them until she pulled them free once more.

"You, only you."

She cried out, lifting her hips for a moment before she thrust down onto his rigid cock, claiming it, drawing it deeply into her body as she rocked. Her sex rippled, holding him, releasing only to clamp tightly on his shaft once more.

His thighs tensed, heels digging into the bedding, his body arched as she shuddered atop of him.

"Wait." She groaned.

He whimpered, struggling to keep control of his hungry body. Each deep lunge of her hips pushed him higher and still he held on, begging with his eyes, the strain playing openly across his naked form.

"Wait." She whispered, cupping her breasts, lifting them, pinching lightly at her own swollen nipples. The coral tips ached for his touch, his lips, those soft nibbling kisses she knew he could bestow when given the chance. She sucked in on her bottom lip, trying to find a moment of focus even as her control threatened to struggle free.

"Please."

She shook her head, her hips now still, but her inner walls were another matter. They tightened, massaging the length of his cock, milking him.

"Mistress!"

Pleasure rippled through her core, claiming her body, mind, and soul as she screamed out. "Now!"

Heat. His. Hers. It didn't matter. Pleasure ruled the moment. She rested her hands against his chest, her nails digging into his taut flesh and still her hips danced, demanding one more cry, one last shudder of pleasure until she was left lying atop of him, his cock still buried between her thighs.

"Mine." She whispered against his neck.

Others would have wanted soft words of love, whispered promises but for him that one word was enough. And for her…

"Yes, Mistress." His breath tickled her ear.

Sue smiled, rocking her hips one last time as he groaned in pleasure and horror combined. Did he fear that she would sit back up and tease his still-hard cock, force another wave of pleasure through his body? Or did he just hope she would push him to the edge one more time?

She sat up, trailing her fingertips down his chest as he shuddered, his eyes glazed, lips parted as he sucked in ragged breaths. A wicked smile claimed her lips even as her hips began their slow dance once more.

*Yes, Mistress.*

What else did she need to hear?

## Terri Pray

Terri Pray is a stay at home wife and mother currently living in Iowa with her second husband. She was born in England, only moving to the States in 1999. They have two children together and share a love of writing and role-playing that brought them together via the Internet. Together they not only run a chat site, Dark Fantasy Chat, but also work in the RPG industry and Terri can often be seen at such conventions as ValleyCon, Gen Con and Origins at the Final Sword Production booth.

Visit Terri on the Web at www.terripray.com.